#3 MILLION DOLLAR GAMBLE

by

Chassie L. West

Programming by Susan M. Zakar

A Parachute Press Book

SCHOLASTIC INC.
New York Toronto London Auckland Sydney Tokyo

Designed by Gene Siegel

ISBN 0-590-33167-1

12 11 10 9 8 7 6 5 4 3 2 1 7 4 5 6 7 8 9/8

Printed in the U.S.A. 01

Warning: The following information is crucial to the success of your mission. Read it carefully. It may save your life.

As a certified member of ACT (the Adventure Connection Team), your job, as always, is to defend the cause of good against evil. It won't be easy, because BRUTE (the Bureau of Random Unlawful Terror and Evil), the international organization bent on wreaking havoc throughout the world, will be fighting you every step of the way. Your computer expertise will be vital to this mission. So turn on your home system. Throughout this adventure you'll be called upon to program it to get the ACT team out of some really tough spots.

Look for the chart next to the program instructions. It will tell you which micros will run each program. If the program won't run as is on your computer, consult the Reference Manual in the back of the book — fast! Good luck. This message will be erased from memory in 30 seconds.

CHAPTER 1

Beep! Beep! Beep! Beep!

Your eyes snap open, but it takes a moment for your brain to power up.

Beep! Beep!

Your computer is signaling an incoming message. Terrific! Bet it's Robin, your new computer buddy, with some weird bug in a program he's working on. And a problem in BASIC is more fun than a problem in algebra any day of the week.

You scrub the sleep from your eyes, shove your homework aside, and blink the monitor into focus. Hey! What's Robin doing? Looks like his fingers are on the wrong keys. His message is pure garbage. Garbage?!!

Suddenly you're wide awake and on your feet. That's not Robin, that's a coded message from ACT! They want you!

TBVNYDZCAKW JWUGG YXVSJBXG FB BWTX ZTJO XDJMP WTV TWCL HRNX HDZZKCAI XGAVVT DKVV CAD VWAUCCK

Hands shaking with excitement, you unlock your desk and pull out the code manual — the latest issue of Marvel Comics' *X-Men*. It might look like an ordinary comic book, but it's not. Place a special decoder sheet over the next to the last page and a short BASIC program springs into view. That — and this month's password, "OPAL" — are all you need to decode the message.

Type the following program into your computer, and run it. Then enter the password and the coded message one line at a time in all capital letters. Lines 50 and 60 should each be typed as one line on your computer.

PROGRAM 1

```
10 REM ENCODER/DECODER
20 P$ = " "
30 PRINT "ENTER YOUR PASSWORD"
40 INPUT K$
50 PRINT "TYPE EACH LINE OF SECRET
   MSG"
60 PRINT "(JUST TYPE 'STOP' WHEN
   DONE)"
70 INPUT C$
80 IF C$ = "STOP" THEN 270
```

```
 90 FOR I = 1 TO LEN(C$)
100 I$ = MID$(C$,I,1)
110 IF ( I$ >= "A") * (I$ <= "Z") THEN 140
120 P$ = P$ + I$
130 GOTO 230
140 J = J + 1
150 IF J <= LEN(K$) THEN 170
160 J = 1
170 K = ASC(MID$(K$,J,1)) – ASC("A") + 1
180 C = ASC(I$) – ASC("A") + 1
190 IF K > C THEN 210
200 K = K + 26
210 P = K – C
220 P$ = P$ + CHR$(P + ASC("A") – 1)
230 NEXT I
240 PRINT P$
250 P$ = " "
260 GOTO 70
270 END
```

IBM	Apple		Radio Shack		Commodore		TI	Atari
PC & PCjr	II+	IIe	TRS-80	Color	64	VIC-20	99/4A	400/800
✓	✓	✓	✓	✓	✓	✓		

This program will run on all the personal computers checked in the chart above. See the Reference Manual, page 113, for changes for the TI and Atari.

A BRUTE agent in your shopping center? No one's safe with BRUTE in this solar system. It gives you the creeps thinking of BRUTE in your neighborhood. And ACT wants you to check it out alone — without a backup. It's one thing being part of a team rocketing off to space stations or trekking into a jungle to fight BRUTE. But going out there alone with no backup? You're a computer expert — not a one-person army!

But orders are orders. ACT must feel it's something you can handle on your own. So, tucking your portable ACT minicomputer in the pocket of your windbreaker, you power down your home terminal and leave. But boy, you do *not* want to go!

It's a typical Saturday at the Gold Star Shopping Center — crowded and busy. You've been here many times when it was packed back to front, and it's never bothered you before. But today you feel frightened.

Look normal, look normal, you keep telling yourself. You detour around the computer store and stop at the Hobby Shop to pick up some balsa wood, spray paint, and glue for the model space station you're building. That's normal, isn't it?

You cover the whole area twice. There is nothing special to see. Whatever the sneaky BRUTEs are pulling, they're doing a pretty good job of hiding it.

Duty done, you're ready to head for home to report in when you remember the supermarket. It's off from the rest of the stores, but it's still part of the shopping center. So you'd better check it out.

You sprint across the two-lane roadway that separates the market from the main section of Gold Star and enter the side door of the Grocery Mart. The place is a mob scene. BRUTE could be holding target practice in there and no one would notice.

You work your way up and down a maze of aisles booby-trapped with stacks of cans and boxes. Running a gauntlet of shopping carts, you pick up a jar of peanut butter so it will look as if you have a reason to be there, and head for the express checkout line. Once there, your elbow hits a big cardboard sign at the end of the counter. Steadying it to keep it from falling over, you see the big red letters at the top: LOTTERY! Then you remember the ticket!

That was a nice little mystery that had perked up a rather dull week. The lottery ticket came in the mail in a plain white envelope. No return address on it. Inside with the ticket was a note, unsigned, but written by a kid, you're sure. The note said to hang on to the ticket, and that winning numbers are posted each Saturday.

Well, it's Saturday and you're here, so you might as well check on the results.

The winning numbers are tacked up on

a board outside the manager's office. You struggle into the crowd, trying to get close enough to see the numbers. The lady next to you gives you an elbow in the side that nearly bends you in half. And there's a kid standing in the cart behind you who keeps belting you between the shoulder blades when his mother isn't looking. But finally you're close enough to see.

You hold your breath, cross your fingers. Your number is 2407. There are two columns of winners — one for free groceries for a month, the other for cash prizes. No 2407. Your hunch was so strong. You start to crumple the ticket into a ball.

But there's a number at the very bottom of the sign. You can't quite see it; someone's in the way. You maneuver a bit closer. It says: GRAND PRIZE WINNER. You squint to make out the number. No. It couldn't be. It is! 2407! "I *got* it! Two-four-oh-seven! *I got it!!*" you yell.

Wriggling your way past smiling faces, you try to show the ticket to the manager. He's new and you don't recognize him, but the sign says his name is Jones. He scowls at you as if it's his own personal money you've won. Then he grabs the phone and dials frantically. You don't care whom he's calling. You're too busy thinking of all the things the money will buy — a new micro, maybe a hard-disk drive. . .

The assistant manager, good old Mr. Clancy, comes out of the little glass cubicle and checks your ticket. "Yes, indeed, you do have it," he shouts into the store's public address system. "Folks, we've got us a Grand Prize winner here!" He, at least, seems very happy about it.

Suddenly you're surrounded by excited shoppers. "Smile!" Mr. Clancy yells, and a flashbulb goes off in your face. "That's for our bulletin board. Now, don't go away!" he says cheerily. "Someone from the newspapers and TV will be coming to interview you."

(. . . a remote controller you can connect with your computer to turn on. . . .) Television? Newspapers? Your head comes down from the clouds *fast*. You remember ACT's instructions: "Keep a low profile." And now you're about to get your face blasted all over the TV tube! Boy, have you *blown* it!

You pull the assistant manager aside. "Look, sir, I'd rather not be interviewed. Honest. Can I just have the money and go?"

His face falls. "No interview? You're sure? Well, if that's the way you feel." He goes into the office and brings back an envelope. "This is a letter to the bank. Don't lose it; all it says is that the bearer is entitled to a check, drawn on our account, for $25,000."

You thank him and wonder what to do next. Everyone is staring at you and smiling. The news is zinging up and down the aisles. You might as well be in a spotlight with your name on a marquee out front. Better report in to ACT pronto. But you need someplace where you won't be noticed.

You run through the store, searching. Finally, hunching down behind a display of large potted palms, you pull out the miniature computer ACT supplies and you log on.

"Password," it demands.

You key in "Orion," your code name.

"Proceed with message."

You explain the situation and hope whoever's on duty understands that you really didn't win on purpose.

It seems a long time before an answer comes. "Wait at rear of store. You will be picked up. Use lunar password." ACT logs off.

Sighing with relief, you make your way to the back door, wondering what kind of transport they'll send. In the past, you've ridden in newspaper trucks and ambulances.

Suddenly, a long black limousine glides up to the curb and a chauffeur — hat, uniform, and all — gets out and comes in the door. He's a huge bruiser with muscles big enough to make the Hulk think twice.

"You the kid who won the Grand Prize? Winner gets a free limo ride home," he says. "Let's go." He's got a weird, thin voice.

You follow him out to the car. What a smart idea, another one of ACT's acts to get an agent from one place to another. A ride in a limousine would be just the kind of "extra" a company sponsoring a contest might offer.

One foot is in the back door when you remember you haven't followed routine. "There's a full moon tonight," you say.

The driver, opening his door, turns to look at you. "So? You a werewolf?"

Your heart begins to beat madly. He's *not* from ACT or he would have answered, "And tomorrow night, too." "Uh — I changed my mind," you stammer, edging away from him.

"That so?" he says.

"Yeah. I — I forgot. I called my father and he's picking me up."

He shakes his head. "Uh-uh. You ain't called nobody. Now, get in the car." He opens his jacket to show a huge gun.

A hold-up! You swallow hard, your mouth dry. Well, you're no dummy. If he wants the letter to the bank, he gets the letter to the bank. You take the envelope from your pocket and extend it toward him. "Here. Take it."

He doesn't even glance at it. "Get in the car." It comes out slow and mean.

"It's the same as a check, honest. All you have to do is take it to the bank and they'll give you the money." Fingers trembling, you take the letter out of the envelope and turn it around so he can count all the zeroes.

He's not impressed. His response is to point the gun at you. "You're wasting my time," he says calmly. "Now for the last time, kid, *get in the car!*"

CHAPTER 2

So here you are, stuck in the backseat of this velvet-padded prison on wheels. You can't get out on the driver's side because there's a steady stream of traffic. You can't get out on the curb side because the driver is leaning against your door as he talks to someone you can't see. You need a plan. Once he gets in and locks these doors, you're dead. Unless, somehow. . . .

You clutch the bag from the Hobby Shop with sweaty hands and a glimmer of a plan flashes in your head. Maybe, just maybe . . . if he'll just keep talking for a few more minutes.

Hands shaking, you dig the tube of glue from the bag, remove the top, and break the seal.

Leaning over the front seat, you work as rapidly as you can, smearing glue on the seat, the steering wheel, and the door handle. You do as thorough a job as you can. Now all you have to do is wait for the glue to set — and for the driver to get into the car.

You look through the window to see what's keeping him. He's talking to that Mr. Jones, the supermarket manager, who certainly looks a lot happier now. Are the two of them in this together? Finally their conversation ends and Mr. Jones goes back into the store. You hold your breath and sit so still, you feel like a department-store dummy.

The driver opens the door and gets in, his right hand on the steering wheel. He reaches over, closes the door, and a funny expression crosses his ugly face. "Huh? Hey! HEY!" That last big "Hey" is when he realizes that one hand is stuck to the door handle and the other is stuck to the wheel.

"You sneaky little — What is this stuff?"

You open the back door and get out. "Atlas glue. Bonds anything to anything — forever." You lean in to give him one last message. "And I wouldn't try to pull my hands away if I were you or you'll be leaving a whole lot of skin behind."

"Wait a minute, wait a minute," he babbles. "You can't leave me here like this!" He tries to free his hand from the steering wheel. "Ow!" he yelps.

"I told you," you say as you take off. You turn back and see him blow the horn with his chin. Signaling for help, you guess. You also guess he must not have seen the shine of the Atlas glue on the horn rim. So there he sits, stuck to the car at three points.

"*JONES!!*" You can still hear him roaring like a bull as you walk rapidly down to the end of the row of stores, turn left, and spot a phone booth. If it's good enough for Superman, it's good enough for you. There's no way to know how much time the glue has bought you, but you think ACT ought to know that someone tried to kidnap you.

Closing yourself into the booth, you dig your ACT computer from your pocket again and log on. Raising your head to peek out, you see Mr. Jones run around the corner, clearly looking for you. You type in, "HELP!"

"On the way," comes back immediately.

It's hot in there with the door closed. But closed in or not, you still feel exposed. You can see out and everybody can see in.

Mr. Jones has disappeared for the moment, but suppose he comes back, looking more carefully this time? He'll be looking for a kid in a navy windbreaker. You shrug out of it quickly, roll it up, and tuck it between your knees. You grab the phone, cradle it between shoulder and ear, and turn your back as if deep in conversation.

Someone raps on the door. It couldn't be the driver. There's no way he could have gotten himself unglued this fast. Besides, he wouldn't be polite enough to knock at the door; he would just break it down with his pinkie. Ignoring the rapping, you begin talking a mile a minute, until a face comes into view.

"Orion! Will you hang up and come on out of there?" You stare, wide-eyed, into the anxious face of Hot Wheels, or H.W. for short. No need for that business about the full moon now. He's picked you up before.

Opening the door, you croak, "Boy, am I glad to see you! I thought my number was up for sure."

H.W. snorts. "If you don't move it, it may be up yet. Let's go!"

"What are you driving?" you ask, trotting behind him.

H.W. doesn't answer. In a moment, you see why, as he waves you around to the passenger side of — oh, no — a garbage truck! But this is no time to be picky. You scramble in, slam the door behind you, and scrunch down under the front seat.

"Don't knock it," H.W. says tersely, shoving the monster into first gear. "It's the only thing we could find at such short notice. What's happening? Tracer said you're in some kind of trouble."

"A man dressed like a chauffeur pulled a gun on me and tried to kidnap me."

H.W. looks at you from the corners of his eyes. "You're kidding. How'd you get away?"

H.W. roars with laughter when you tell

him about the glue. "But I figure that won't hold him for very long," you warn him.

"Well, let's just check and see. Where's he parked?"

"Around to the right behind the supermarket. You sure this is a good idea?" you ask.

"I want to eyeball anyone who comes after one of our people with a gun. Besides, they won't look for you in a garbage truck," H.W. responds, his voice deadly quiet. "Big black limo?"

"That's it."

"I know the face," he says soberly. "Name's Gressom. He's a gorilla. You *were* in trouble."

"I may still be. What's happening?" you ask.

"There's somebody in the car with him now, in the backseat. Baldheaded dude. Looks like he's pouring something over Gressom's hands. And a clerk is coming out with several bottles of — nail-polish remover, I think."

"That's probably what it is. It dissolves the glue. He'll be free any minute. Shouldn't we move a little faster?"

"We're almost out of the parking lot. After that . . . uh-oh." Eyes narrowed, H.W. peers into the sideview mirror. "I don't know why, but the baldheaded guy's watching us. Your buddy must be loose now." H.W.'s expression is grim. "The car's moving, trying to make a U-turn. You okay down there?" All you can do is nod. It's hard to talk with a lump the size of a cantaloupe stuck in your throat. "Yup, he's coming out the same way we did."

"Uh, is this thing souped up? A special engine or something?" you ask.

"Well, it's not the engine the Department of Sanitation put in it — we've done some tinkering of our own — but as heavy as this baby is, it can only go so fast."

"Then what are we going to do?" you ask. Your rescue vehicle begins to feel like a prison. "There's no way you can outrun a car like that."

"Hey, give me some credit," H.W. protests. "They don't call me Hot Wheels for nothing. I'll get us out of this. Just hang on."

You're reassured by the "us," but otherwise the trip is about as awful as any you've ever had. The worst part is not being able to see. And H.W. is too busy watching traffic in front of him and the limo behind him to give progress reports. But from the way he keeps eyeing his sideview mirror, you *know* the limo is still on your tail. But why? What gave you away?

H.W. digs in his pocket, pulls out a small black box, and begins to talk into it. It's the first time you've seen the new communicators ACT just distributed.

"You calling for help?" you ask hopefully.

He looks at you with surprise. "We don't

need any help. Everything's under control. Just a slight change in plans. We'll have to pick up Tracer."

"Who's Tracer?" you ask.

"He's in charge of the surveillance operation. I just filled him in on our buddy back there in the limo. Tracer thinks he'd better talk to you as soon as possible. He's a good guy. You'll like him."

"Sure," you say. You'll love him like a brother if he can help you get away from the gorilla in the limo.

You've got a cramp in your right leg, so you try to squirm into a more comfortable position. That's when you see it. In the rush to get into the truck, your windbreaker didn't make it all the way. Half of it is bunched against the side of the passenger seat; the other half is caught under the door — and it's trailing along the street! That's how they found you. You've blown it again!

"H.W., it's my jacket. That's how he knows I'm in here."

"Huh?"

You explain, your face crumpling with dismay. "It's all my fault. I'm sorry."

H.W. seems to shrug it off. "Don't sweat it, Orion. It could have happened to anyone. Besides, I've figured out how to get rid of him for a while — at least long enough for us to pick up Tracer and get the two of you to one of our emergency hideouts. Hang on."

The warning comes just in time for you to brace yourself. The truck grinds to a stop and H.W. struggles with a gear shift he hasn't used before. The truck begins to shake.

"What's going on?"

H.W.'s grin is half a block wide. "Nothing. Just getting rid of some garbage."

It's a second before you catch on. You push up far enough to get a good look. H.W. has stopped in the middle of the entrance to a parking lot. The rear of the vehicle that holds the dumpster rises slowly from its foundation, tilts backward, and you can hear the sound of its full load tumbling out.

What a sight! The hood and front windshield of the big black limo are disappearing under a ton of eggshells, fish heads, rotting vegetables, and all sorts of awful, smelly stuff. The limo can't back up because there is a long line of cars behind it honking like mad. It's trapped under a mountain of garbage.

"One last thing for good measure," H.W. says. He reverses the small lever and the dumpster tumbles free of the long metal arms holding it. It lands on top of the garbage on top of the limo. "That ought to give us some maneuvering room." He shifts into first gear and you're off again.

The last thing you see before the truck turns a corner is the driver glaring at the dumpster that is sitting on the hood of the limo. And, boy, does he look mad!

CHAPTER 3

This seems to be your day for visiting shopping centers. H.W. drives to one about ten blocks from the Gold Star and maneuvers the garbage truck toward a lone dumpster sitting at the end of a loading platform. There's no traffic at the moment, just a few delivery trucks and a parked tractor trailer.

"Get out and go back to the dumpster," H.W. says. "There's a sliding door on the rear of it. Open it and get in."

"In the *dumpster*?" you ask, remembering the load in the last one.

H.W. grins. "Trust me."

You climb out, leaving your ruined windbreaker behind, and dart back to the dumpster. There's barely enough room between the rear of it and the brick wall behind it, but you squeeze through. You open the door, put one leg over the threshold, and freeze.

''Holy smoke,'' you whisper. A dark-haired man with black eyes that sort of burn into you is standing just inside, but you'll get to him in a minute. You're too busy admiring the interior of this thing.

It's the Cadillac of dumpsters! Not only is it carpeted with dark-green pile an inch deep, it's also paneled and has padded seats around three sides. There's a desk attached to the fourth wall and above it a console.

''We use this as a command post for stakeouts. Pretty good accommodations, wouldn't you say?'' the man asks, so that you have to turn and focus on him.

''I'll say!'' Then you remember routine. You don't plan to flunk that test twice in one day. ''There's a full moon tonight,'' you murmur, feeling a little silly.

The man smiles. ''Tomorrow night, too. Come on in, Orion. I'm Tracer.'' He closes the sliding door behind you. ''Better settle down and brace yourself,'' he suggests quickly, as he sits down himself. You follow his lead, just in time. There is an ear-splitting clang of metal on metal, and the room begins to rock.

''Hey! What's going on?'' you cry.

''H.W.'s taking us to one of our emergency substations,'' Tracer replies. ''I could have gotten in the truck with you, but the engine's noisy and we need to talk.'' You swallow hard, trying to keep your cool as the enclosure rocks back and forth. ''We're almost up,'' he says soothingly. At those words, the dumpster settles down with a thump.

He crosses to the console and flips a switch. ''Can you hear okay, H.W.?'' he asks.

''Loud and clear,'' the driver's voice comes back, a metallic quality to it. ''This new headset's really neat.''

''Okay, Orion,'' Tracer says. ''I already know about your orders from ACT. There are seven BRUTE agents in the area and we could round up only six of our guys for surveillance. That's the reason you were pressed into service. Tell me what happened. Something about winning a lottery?''

You run through the whole episode for him, making a detour at one point to explain how you received the lottery ticket.

''And it was a winner,'' Tracer says. ''Interesting. By the way, that was quick thinking with the glue. What'd this chauffeur look like?''

''I can answer that one for him, boss,'' H.W. says. ''I saw him. It was Gressom.''

Tracer's face hardens into cold, flat planes. ''Oliver Gressom. A muscle man for BRUTE. We had a tail on him until he pulled a slip on us a little while ago. That must have been when he went to get the limo.''

You're glad you're sitting down, because your legs turn to Jello. You should have known the driver might be a BRUTE agent. Why was he after you?

Tracer asks the same thing. "Gressom's been keeping a low profile. Why would he expose himself to try to kidnap you? Obviously BRUTE sent him. Why?"

"I don't know," you whisper.

"Well, I won't insult you by asking if you've told anyone about your activities with us," Tracer continues. "But have you done anything different lately? Anything that might tip off your connection with us?"

"No, sir." You can answer that readily enough. Everything's been the same as usual.

"Met anyone new or made any new friends?"

"No, sir. Oh, except Robin, and he doesn't count because I've never really met him. He's a computer buddy."

"A what?"

"There's this network bulletin board that a lot of us kids use. Robin left a message on it that he had a really tough programming problem and needed help. I thought it might be interesting, so I called him. That's how it started."

"And since then?"

"He's called maybe once a week with a new problem — we call them 'stumpers' — and I work on it and call him back with the answer. It's been fun."

"Boss," H.W.'s voice cuts in. "I think we've picked up a tail."

You can see Tracer tense up. "Deal with

it,'' he snaps sharply. ''Keep talking,'' he says to you. ''What kind of problems have you and this Robin been working on?''

''Just programming stuff. He's a whiz with computer languages, knows more than I do.''

''How long has this been going on?''

''Two or three months, I guess. We've gotten to be pretty good friends.''

''Must have been wrong,'' H.W. announces. ''Nobody back there now.''

The tension drains from Tracer's face. ''Well,'' he says to you, ''we'll have to check him out.''

''Robin? Why?''

''He's the only unknown quantity in your life.''

You examine his idea from all angles and come up with the same answer each time. ''No, Tracer, he couldn't have anything to do with BRUTE. He's just a kid!''

''So are you,'' Tracer reminds you. ''If he's as good as you say, why couldn't BRUTE use him as one of their computer aces, the same way ACT uses you?''

''Because he'd tell them to go empty their buffers, that's why. In fact, Robin's hero is Robin Hood. He was a good guy, wasn't he?''

''The Sheriff of Nottingham might not have thought so,'' Tracer remarks dryly. ''What's your Robin's name and address so I can run the check on him?''

"I don't know." Even though that's not unusual, you suspect Tracer's not going to like it. "Robin may not even be his real name. Some kids give themselves other names, like CB monikers. All I know is the telephone number for his computer line."

Tracer's face looks as if it's been carved out of ice. "When it comes right down to it, you can't even be sure he's a kid, can you?"

You're stumped. How do you explain why you feel so strongly about something when there's no proof to back you up?

"Let me call him. I bet all I have to do is ask and he'll tell us anything you want."

Tracer thinks it over. "Why don't you do that?" he says finally. "I'd be interested to see how he reacts to hearing from you. If he's with BRUTE, he'll expect you to be in their clutches. If he asks where you are, that may mean he knows they botched the job and he'll be trying to pinpoint your location for them."

"He won't ask," you assure him. "Do you think it's all right if I link up with an ACT computer and have it make the call?"

"Go ahead."

Powering up the tiny unit, you key in the instructions, then Robin's phone number, and wait. The one message you didn't expect fills the screen of your monitor. "UNABLE TO COMPLETE CALL." Robin's not on-line. You slump in disappointment. The only thing you can do is leave a message for him on the network bulletin board to be on-line at a certain time.

You key in the number of the bulletin board, your account number, and password, and discover that there's a message waiting on it for you. The first line of it makes you sit up and grin. It looks like garbage, but isn't. It's in code, one you worked on with Robin.

XNCQN JMZF. JDSL'NS QXJSN TS. UBNNL QABMJ JDS VBJJSNL. C YR TY. LRNM'JN UELNJ !N. B LRBTV BL'W GNIUCWN YE LRN SBTTBTD LBIVNL B WNTL MYC. DYL LY RBXN. JYGBT.

You instruct the mini to save the message and hope you can remember the program to decode it.

"So what's happening?" Tracer asks.

"He wasn't on-line, but he left a message for me on the bulletin board. Give me a minute, okay? I need to decode it."

"Decode it?" Tracer echoes. "Why would he leave a message in code?"

"Probably just to give me something to do," you respond with a smile and get down to the job at hand. After a few tries, you finally remember the program. It's a code you called QWERTYCODE.

Type the following program into your computer (type lines 20 and 30 each as one line) and run it. Then type in Robin's message, in capital letters, one line at a time. Don't be surprised if you can't decode all of the message — life isn't always that simple. If you can, save this program.

IMPORTANT: After you've run the decoder, save the part of the message that is still garbled, either in your computer or by copying it onto a piece of paper.

PROGRAM 2

```
 10 REM QWERTYCODE
 20 DATA "QAZWSXEDCRFVTGBYH
    NUJMIKOLP"
 30 DATA "ABCDEFGHIJKLMNOPQRS
    TUVWXYZ"
 40 READ A$,B$
 50 PRINT "TYPE 'STOP' TO END PROGRAM"
 60 PRINT
 70 PRINT "INPUT MESSAGE";
 80 INPUT C$
 90 IF C$ = "STOP" THEN 210
100 FOR I = 1 TO LEN(C$)
110 D$ = MID$(C$,I,1)
120 FOR J = 1 TO 26
130 IF D$ = MID$(A$,J,1) THEN 170
140 NEXT J
150 PRINT D$;
160 GOTO 180
170 PRINT MID$(B$,J,1);
```

```
180 NEXT I
190 PRINT
200 GOTO 70
210 END
```

IBM	Apple		Radio Shack		Commodore		TI	Atari
PC & PCjr	II+	IIe	TRS-80	Color	64	VIC-20	99/4A	400/800
✓	✓	✓	✓	✓	✓	✓		

This program will run on all the personal computers checked in the chart above. See the Reference Manual, page 115, for changes for TI and Atari.

You feel a cold chill at the back of your neck and your stomach begins to knot. The part of the message you can read is frightening enough. But even decoded, you can't understand the rest of it. It's garbled, as if it's in another kind of code. It certainly isn't anything the two of you worked on. Why would Robin do that? And what does he mean by "They're after me"?

You look up. "Robin's in trouble."

"He sure is," Tracer says grimly. "With me, for one. Sorry about the lottery, is he? Sure, he is. That double-crossing little creep set you up!"

CHAPTER 4

''Tracer, listen,'' you begin, still unwilling to believe the worst about your friend. ''Robin wouldn't — '' You shut up and grab the edge of your seat as the dumpster begins to rock like a gondola on a ferris wheel. Your stomach churns at the motion and you close your eyes as the dumpster comes down hard.

Tracer flips off all the switches on the console. ''Follow me,'' he says shortly. He steps out. You're in a garage filled with delivery vans. H.W. follows and gives you a thumbs up sign as he gets into one of the vans and drives out. You hate to see him go. At least he seemed to be on your side. The garage doors slide closed.

''What is this place?'' you ask.

''As far as the outside world is concerned, it's a fur storage warehouse, but it's really one of ACT's emergency shelters.''

You trail him from the empty garage area through a small office. At the rear of the office is a large, round, metal door like the ones you've seen on bank vaults. Tracer steps through it into a small, high-ceilinged room where furs hang from top to bottom, wall-to-wall. It's very cold. You wish you had your windbreaker.

Tracer presses a button in the rear wall. Machinery begins to purr. The whole wall, furs and all, slides open to expose an even larger console than the one in the dumpster and a bank of computers and several terminals.

Tracer's communicator crackles. "Boss," H.W. calls. There's a strange urgency in his voice. "Something's happening."

The dark-haired man moves quickly to the console and pushes two buttons. "What?"

H.W.'s baritone fills the room from one of the speakers on the console. "I intercepted some conversation between our guys on the other channel. The BRUTE crew's leaving, all of them. They must have gotten a signal or something. They seem to be headed out of town."

"Tell our guys not to lose them," Tracer snaps. "And keep me posted."

"Will do, boss. Over and out."

"What's Robin's computer phone number?" Tracer asks abruptly.

You rattle it off for him as he flips switches on another part of the console. He requests any information ACT can dig up on your computer pal.

"Tracer, I know you don't believe me, but Robin's clean," you insist. "I'm scared stiff that something's happened to him. He's got half the message in one code and the second half in another I don't even know! That's not like him!"

"Maybe he was just trying to make it look good," Tracer suggests. "Let's see it." You hand him your mini with the message from Robin still on the monitor. "What's with this 'Friar Tuck' business?"

"I told you, his hero is Robin Hood. He calls me Little John. It just means I'm a friend. Are we going to help him?"

"First, we're going to find out who he is, where he is, and what he's been doing," Tracer says. "*Then* maybe we'll help him. And that 'maybe' depends on a lot of things, like, for instance, if he really needs the help, which I doubt. Now excuse me, Orion, I have to check on my men." He goes back to the console to contact the other ACT operatives in the area.

It's so frustrating not being able to convince Tracer that Robin is innocent! Maybe you can track down the information about him.

"Tracer, can I use one of these computers?"

"Help yourself," he answers, not really paying attention.

You call the network bulletin board again.

Your luck is holding; the systems operator on duty is someone you know.

"Sandi, this is an emergency. I need the name and address of the computer pal who left the message for me today."

She responds: "Nobody left a message for you today."

You scowl. "Yes, they did. I received it a few minutes ago. It's still there. Looks like a bunch of junk. Please check."

"Why didn't you say so?" Sandi comes back. "That wasn't sent today. It's been on here since last night."

You look horrified at that. "Are you sure? Last night?"

"Yes, I'm sure," she answers. "The message was left at 10:47 P.M. And you know I can't give you the name and address. Against the rules, remember?"

You chew your lip in frustration. If there's any possibility that he's been off-line ever since he left that message, then something is very, very wrong. "I told you this is an emergency," you key in. "I'm not kidding, Sandi. He's really in trouble!"

There is a pause that seems to go on forever. "Member has specifically requested that name not be released without permission," Sandi types in. "But I'll give you the address and telephone number. Will that help?"

Of course it will! She sends the information, which you copy down. Robin lives in

Forestville, a small town on the other side of the Air Force base.

Quietly, you slip the piece of notepaper in front of Tracer. ''Robin's address and phone number,'' you say softly.

''How'd you get it?'' he demands. ''Did you call that kid?''

''The bulletin board gave it to me.''

He switches from the surveillance channel back to HQ. ''Tracer here,'' he barks out. ''This Robin kid lives at 601 Forest Heights Avenue in Forestville. Are there any of our people on the base you could send to do a quick check? Quietly, though. We don't want to give ourselves away.''

''Will do,'' someone responds.

Back on the surveillance channel, H.W. is calling in. ''Boss, six of the BRUTE cars are all headed east on Route 17. Don't know where the seventh is. Blaine lost him.''

''What about Gressom?''

''He's two cars behind me. He's got that Jones character with him in the front seat and there's somebody in the back, too, but I can't see him clearly.''

''Well, don't lose them. Wonder where they're going.''

''To the airport?'' you suggest. There's nothing else out there.

''We can't afford to lose track of these guys,'' Tracer says. ''Something big is up and we've got to find out what. Let's go.''

He steps on a button on the floor and the wall of furs slides back in place, concealing the equipment. He turns to leave and then stops short, a startled expression on his face. You follow his eyes and your mouth drops open. The vault door is closed.

Tracer moves to it quickly and pushes at it, but it's obvious that's useless. "Well, that tears it," he mutters. "Now we know where the seventh BRUTE agent was. That thing didn't close by itself."

"Can't you call somebody to come open it?" you ask.

"I hate to tell you this," he says gently, "but there's a time lock on it and it's not going to open until Monday morning at eight o'clock."

"Monday morning!" you croak.

He gives a short nod. "All these rooms are airtight. By the time that door opens, we'll be dead. I'm sorry, Orion. It looks like BRUTE got to you after all."

"What about calling someone with a blowtorch or something?" you ask, barely hiding the panic in your voice.

Tracer shakes his head. "If anyone tampers with it from the outside, the whole building will explode! That's to make sure no one ever finds any evidence of ACT here. There's no contingency plan for getting out from the inside. I guess they figured an ACT agent wouldn't be dumb enough to get locked in. I'm really sorry, Orion. This is my fault. I didn't do my job."

You try a game smile, but turn away so he won't see how scared you're getting. "No chance of picking the lock from this side, then," you murmur.

"I'm afraid not. The time mechanism's set by computer so that — "

"By computer?" you yell. "You mean that boxy thing in the center of the door is a computer?"

"I guess. I never had to think about it before, so I really don't know."

"If it is the computer, maybe I can do something with it."

You stare at the square thing that seems attached to the middle of the door, tug at it, and feel something move under your hands. It's a metal cover that slips off easily and you're staring at a keyboard that has a calculatorlike keypad at the side. Above it are two tiny display windows. One says, "Monday 0800," the time it will open. The one below has the present day and time.

"What do you think?" Tracer asks.

"If I can cut into the programming, I may be able to speed up the clock." You ask for a listing of the program it uses.

Type the following program into your computer and run it. (Lines 40, 50, 300, and 320 should each be typed as one line on your computer.) As you can see, the clock is running slowly. At this rate, you'll suffocate before you get out. So interrupt the program. This is usually done by hitting the control break, STOP, or similar key.

Now list the program. Can you figure out how to speed up the clock? Hint: Check out line 60. If you're stumped, check page 116 of the Reference Manual for help.

PROGRAM 3

```
10 REM THE VAULT LOCK
20 DATA 6,17,30,00,1
30 READ D,H,M,S,N
40 REM   DAY,HOUR,MINUTE,SECOND,
   INCREMENT
50 D$ = "SUNDAY . . . MONDAY . . . TUESDAY
   . . WEDNESDAYTHURSDAY . FRIDAY . . .
   SATURDAY"
60 C = 10
70 IF C >= 10 THEN 90
80 N = 7
90 HOME
100 FOR T = 1 TO C STEP 1
110 NEXT T
120 S = S + N * N
130 IF S < 60 THEN 160
140 M = M + N * N
150 S = 0
160 IF M < 60 THEN 190
170 M = 0
```

```
180 H = H + 1
190 If H < 24 THEN 240
200 H = 0
210 D = D + 1
220 IF D < 7 THEN 240
230 D = 0
240 VTAB 10: HTAB (10)
250 PRINT "THE VAULT IS CLOSED!"
260 PRINT
270 PRINT TAB(10);"  ";H;":";M;":";S;"  "
280 PRINT
290 PRINT TAB(12); MID$(D$,D * 9 + 1,9)
300 IF ((H <> 8) + (M <> 0) + (S <> 0) +
    (D <> 1)) THEN 100
310 HOME
320 PRINT "MONDAY 08:00 THE VAULT IS
    OPEN"
330 END
```

IBM	Apple		Radio Shack		Commodore		TI	Atari
PC & PCjr	II+	IIe	TRS-80	Color	64	VIC-20	99/4A	400/800
	√	√						

This program will run on all the personal computers checked in the chart above. See the Reference Manual, page 116, for changes for the other systems.

The silence as you work seems deafening. But then gradually you become aware of other sounds: Tracer's breathing, quiet but rapid; the click of the keys of the keyboard; and most of all, the soft *tick-tick* of the internal mechanism, as the numbers on the digital clock spin. It seems to get louder and louder.

Finally you think you have it. "Cross your fingers," you tell Tracer. You begin to type.

Run the program again, this time with the changes that you think will speed up the clock.

Holding your breath, you finally hear it — a very soft *click*. The door moves.

"It worked!" you shout. "It's OH-PENNN!" You pull it open and dart through. "We're out! We're out!"

Tracer, following, beams and extends his hand. "Orion, I owe you one. You saved our lives. We're lucky to have you on our team. Look, about this trip to the airport — "

"I'm ready when you are."

"Well, it might be better if you stayed behind," he suggests. "I have a feeling this is going to be really dangerous."

"I don't care. Robin and I seem to be mixed up in this. I don't know if I got him in trouble or the other way around, but I've got to find out what's going on and prove that Robin's not a traitor!"

Tracer sighs. "Well, okay. Come on."

He goes back into the garage to the far corner and gets into the funniest-looking car you've ever seen.

''What is that?'' you ask. The car is small like a sub-subcompact. It's wedge-shaped and it only has three wheels — one in the front center, two in the rear. There's a kind of bulge in the roof that looks sort of like a trunk.

''Hop in back,'' Tracer says. ''It's experimental and hasn't been approved by ACT yet, but this is an emergency, so — ''

He starts the engine, which is surprisingly quiet. After managing a U-turn in a very tight space, he scoots under the garage door and throws the car in gear. Zoom! You're out on the street and around the corner in a flash.

''Wow! This little thing can move!'' you yell, fastening your seatbelt. Peering at the dashboard, you begin to see why. It's got as many dials as the Space Shuttle.

Tracer pushes a button in the center of the dashboard and the car begins to quiver.

''Uh — Tracer, what's going on?''

''Hold on to your hat,'' he says tersely.

''Hey! There's a — a rotor spinning around up there!'' you yell.

''Of course!'' Tracer shouts. ''Didn't I tell you this thing is called a helicarpter?''

That's about the time you stop trying to figure out what's happening above you and look down — way down. ''Hey, we're flying!''

CHAPTER 5

Since the helicarpter goes 120 miles per hour, you get to the airport in six minutes!

Tracer slows and drops easily to ground level just outside the airport parking lot as if he does this kind of thing every day. He maneuvers into a parking place and is out of the helicarpter and heading toward the nearest door before you're able to move.

You pull yourself together and follow Tracer to the airport security office, where he flashes some kind of I.D. card at the man behind the desk and does some fast talking. After a few moments, he waves you in. "Come on," he says, as he follows the man across the main terminal to a door marked "Maintenance."

Shortly, you find yourself in the overalls and cap of an airport employee. Tracer shoves a pushbroom in your hand. "Make it look good," he says, grinning. "You take one side of the main terminal, I'll take the other. If you see Gressom, come and get me. And keep that cap pulled down over your face. We don't want him to recognize you.''

That's the last thing he has to tell you!

In an hour you know for certain that the one thing you don't want to do the rest of your life is sweep airports. Your arms are about to drop from their sockets, when you see H.W. skirting the edge of the crowd.

He gets a newspaper and sits down, his eyes flitting from one side of the terminal to the other. But Tracer didn't give you instructions about making contact with Hot Wheels, so you just keep sweeping.

It seems half a century later when you're jostled by someone behind you. You look over your shoulder to stare right at your old friend, Oliver Gressom!

He's not alone either; he's with the sour-faced supermarket manager, Mr. Jones, who's pushing a small figure in a wheelchair. But since Gressom's the one who had the gun pointing at your belly button earlier today, he's the one who holds your attention.

''Whyncha look where you're goin'?'' Gressom growls at you and pushes past. Luckily, he doesn't recognize you.

You've got to find Tracer quick. But glancing toward H.W., you see him shaking his head at you and getting to his feet. You hope he's trying to tell you that he'll look for Tracer.

Pushing your broom, you follow Gressom and company, who head for a ticket agent. Suddenly Gressom stops and turns, frowning. He looks right at you!

Lockers hug the wall directly opposite and you head for them, nudging your small pile of debris as if it's gold and you don't want to lose one scrap. Your head is lowered as far as it will go. Hunching your shoulders for good measure, you feel like a turtle trying to pull into its shell.

Gressom, still staring at you, takes a step in your direction.

"Where're you going?" Jones asks.

You keep pushing that broom and heading for the lockers. *Shoop, shoop, shoop.*

Gressom stops and tilts his head to one side. "That kid with the broom . . ."

"What?" his partner snaps. "Come on. Get the tickets and let's go! We're already late for the plane." He leans over to tuck the blanket around the figure in the wheelchair.

You're still sweeping as if your life depends on it, which it just may. *Shoop, shoop, shoop.*

Gressom backs up a step. "Yeah. Guess you're right." He turns away, but all the while he's paying for the tickets he keeps looking at you. You keep right on sweeping.

Finally, he and Jones move away from the counter and begin talking about something else. You slump against the wall, head bowed, and concentrate on trying to stop shaking. It takes a few minutes.

In the meantime, you convince yourself to turn around to keep an eye on them. You also try to get a better look at the figure in the wheelchair, but whoever it is has been covered teeth to toes with a blanket. Bandages prevent you from seeing the person's face.

Before long, Tracer arrives, sauntering along as if he's in no hurry at all. "I see him," he says softly.

"What took you so long?" you ask tensely. "Gressom thought I looked familiar and was about to come over to take a look."

Tracer eyes you sympathetically. "Sorry, Orion. I was at the other end of the terminal. He seems to have forgotten about you now. He's talking to a man pushing a wheelchair."

"Yeah, I know. That's Jones, the manager of the supermarket."

Tracer's narrowed eyes jump to the counter. Frowning, he shakes his head. "Never seen him before. He must be new. I wonder who's in the wheelchair."

"Whoever it is is awfully short. They have any midgets on their team?"

"You never know," he says "They're leaving. Stay here while I see what I can find out."

He ambles toward the counter and looks up at the airline's schedule of departures. He and the attendant talk for a few minutes. As he comes back, H.W. strides over to join you.

"There's only one flight leaving anytime soon," Tracer says softly. "Makes several stops and terminates Solonia. The attendant commented on the unusual number of passengers ticketed to Solonia today, so I assume that's where our boys are heading."

At the risk of sounding stupid, you ask, "Where's Solonia? I've never heard of it."

Tracer smiles. "A lot of people have never heard of it. It's a little three-by-five kingdom in western Europe. They've been having their troubles; the treasury's almost bankrupt. So why is BRUTE going there? And who's in that wheelchair? I don't like it."

"Boss," H.W. says, "I checked in with headquarters to bring them up to date. They want you to contact them. They've got some information for you."

"And I've got some for them," Tracer says grimly, "along with a few questions. But we need a place where we'll have privacy."

"My van?" H.W. offers, jerking a thumb over his shoulder toward the parking lot.

"Meet you there," Tracer says. "Orion and I have to turn in our brooms." He smiles down at you. "Unless you'd rather keep it as a souvenir?"

"You kidding me?" you howl. "I don't care if I never see another broom as long as I live!"

CHAPTER 6

H.W.'s van is a regular panel truck — at least that's what it looks like on the outside. Inside he's got a living room, kitchen, bathroom, bedroom, and an office! The only thing he's missing is a fireplace.

Tracer's been here before and goes directly to H.W.'s communications console to contact headquarters. Since there's nothing for you to do for the moment, you figure it's a good time to work on the second part of Robin's message.

You try every decoding instruction you can think of. Nothing works. You can't understand why Robin changed from one code to another in the middle of the message. A strange code at that.

H.W. pops back in with a couple of sandwiches. "Ham and cheese," he says, "with lettuce and tomato." He glances at the monitor. "Looks like somebody had their fingers on the wrong keys. I do it all the time." He goes out again.

You stare at the screen. Suppose that's what really happened? It's not something Robin would usually do, but if he was as scared as he says, it could have happened and he might not have realized it.

Looking at the keyboard, you figure that he probably had his fingers on the correct row. So the question is, were both hands one key off or just one hand? And in which direction, to his right or left? It takes three tries before you finally hit it. He had shifted one key to the right. All you've got to do is write a program to run on the garbled end of the message, and you'll have it!

Write a program that will decode the rest of the output you got when you decoded Robin's message. If you were able to save the QWERTYCODE in the computer, list it. You should be able to use it as the basis of your new program. HINT: Change the DATA statements. If you need help, see page 119 in the Reference Manual.

"Tracer, this proves it!" you yell. "This proves Robin's on our side! And I was right. He was in real trouble."

H.W. comes back, perhaps hearing the panic in your voice. "What's wrong, Orion?"

He moves behind you to read the monitor. "Hoo, boy. Looks like somebody's in hot water. Is that from your friend?"

"Yes, and this message was sent last night! And they must have gotten him, because he's not on-line and he's *always* on-line!"

H.W. stares at it, frowning. "Orion, if he left it last night, how'd he know you had the winning ticket when you didn't know it yourself until today?"

Shock paralyzes you as the possibilities of what that may mean sink in. "I don't know! *He* sent it to me? I — I don't get this."

H.W. pats you on the shoulder. "Understand, I'm not taking sides, but don't you think it's kind of fishy that *he* sent you the lottery ticket, somehow knowing that it was a winner? And that after you claimed the check, BRUTE tried to snatch you? If I didn't know better, I would swear you'd been set up."

You're disappointed. You had thought you could count on H.W. to be an ally.

Tracer walks over and stares at the monitor. He looks as if he's trying very hard to be fair, but there's steel in his voice. "That message may say a lot of things, Orion. One thing it says for sure is that there *is* a link between Robin and BRUTE. His sending you that ticket is the proof we needed. Also"— his face shows no emotion —"HQ has found out that a notorious BRUTE agent is Chairman of the Board of the corporation that owns the supermarket. They wanted you. You were the fish, the lottery ticket was the bait. You bit and they almost landed you. All thanks to Robin."

"I still don't believe it." But somehow, you don't sound as sure as you did before.

"There are a few other things you should know." Tracer interrupts your thoughts. "HQ ran the check on Robin's telephone activity. He's been calling all over the world, literally. Oddly enough, all those overseas calls have been to computers used for one purpose: they control various lotteries in those countries."

What had Robin been doing?

"Also," Tracer continues, "there are only three local numbers he's called with any regularity. One is yours. The second is the supermarket's lottery computer."

"The programs we were working on . . ." you respond slowly, ". . . the stumpers. He was working out how to break into the program that selects the winners of lottery contests! *That's* how he knew my ticket would win!"

Tracer isn't smiling. There seems to be more bad news. "It took a while to track the third telephone number. It appeared to be local, except that calls to that number were forwarded to a second number that was *not* local. Then the second number forwarded it on to a third. ACT tracked it to its final destination — overseas. Solonia."

You have a sinking feeling in the pit of your stomach. "But he thought he was calling a local number," you remind Tracer, knowing you're skating on thin ice.

"Possibly," Tracer says. "But how can we be sure? We've checked at Robin's home. Last name's Gold, by the way. The results of an examination of his computer room are what I'm getting to. The wire between the phone jack and his modem had been cut."

"Cut?" you gasp. "Then that proves somebody snatched him. He would never have cut his own line. He didn't get away last night." Tracer and H.W. are exchanging pointed looks. "What's going on? What are you two thinking?" you demand. Suddenly you know. "The person in the wheelchair," you whisper, remembering how small the figure seemed, and even more chilling, how very, very still.

You jump up. "Tracer, BRUTE's *got* him. We have to rescue him. We've just got to!"

"Calm down," he responds, squeezing your shoulder. "We intend to. HQ is already working on a team to go and — "

"I want to go. I've *got* to go!"

Tracer's mouth turns down at the corners. "We assumed there'd be no way to convince you to stay here. You're on the team. So am I. But I have to tell you, Orion, I'm not sure whether your friend will want to be rescued. He may be with them because he chooses to be."

"I don't believe it and never will," you announce stubbornly. "When do we go?"

"The next plane leaves tomorrow —"

"That's too late," you protest.

"Nothing we can do about it. And it gives us time to work up a rescue plan, so settle down. Here." He tears the bottom off the sheet on which he has written his notes. "That's the phone number in Solonia. One of the first things we have to do when we get there is trace it. Put it in your computer so it won't get lost."

"That's the longest phone number I've ever seen," you mutter.

H.W. snorts. "That's Solonia. They don't do anything like anyone else. Other countries use 10 numbers. Solonia? They've got to have something like 15 numbers. Nuttiest place in the world." He leaves to close the kitchen.

Distracted, you decide to make a project out of it, just to have something to do. While Tracer and H.W. are conferring, you key in a program you made up to help you remember phone numbers. It translates the numbers into the corresponding letters on the telephone dial, then it combines them into words.

The computer takes a long time to work it out. When it's finally finished, you almost wish you had simply memorized the telephone number. The telephone number in Solonia has been translated by your computer to read: BRUTE HEADQUARTERS.

CHAPTER 7

You spend a sleepless night in the van. For the first time, you're having serious doubts about Robin yourself. He seemed like such a good kid — he couldn't be a BRUTE agent. Or could he?

You're glad when Tracer tells you to get ready for the briefing. Nothing has gone according to procedure on this mission. Somehow the idea of a formal briefing is comforting. Still, you are taken aback when you meet the man who is going to conduct the session.

He is the biggest man you've ever seen. He's got a reddish-brown complexion, a jutting nose you could hang your coat on, and glossy black hair. And when he stands up — and up and up and up — the room seems to shrink. He's almost seven feet tall, with wall-to-wall shoulders.

''Orion,'' he rumbles, with a smile as

gentle as a baby's. "My name is Walking High As Mountain. My teammates call me the Chief. I'm the coordinator of the sector this month."

"Pleased to meet you," you murmur, thinking how wimpy that sounds.

"Anything new to report?" the Chief asks Tracer.

"Not really. Except that Orion's ready to go. Right now."

The Chief nods kindly. "I understand. You are concerned about your friend. You are convinced that this Robin *is* your friend?" he asks softly.

"Yes, sir. I *know* he is."

The Chief's dark eyes rest on you for a moment. He nods. "Robin is fortunate to have such a friend as you. Take a seat. I must tell you of our plans and introduce you to the third member of your team for this mission. Where did he go?" The Chief starts for the door.

"Right here." A soft voice stops him.

A figure rises from a couch at the other end of the room. He was there all the time and you hadn't noticed him. As he crosses to join the three of you, you begin to understand why. He is the most colorless, unremarkable person you've ever seen. Pale skin, pale eyes, brownish hair. A face that's just a face, absolutely nothing special about it. And he's not tall, not short, not anything.

"Tracer, Orion," the Chief rumbles,

''your teammate — code name, the Chameleon.''

The Chameleon ducks his head and peers at you shyly as he shakes your hand with a grip that wouldn't make a dent in a cotton ball. ''Pleased,'' he murmurs.

Tracer beams at him. ''You were the one who got us out of that bit of trouble in South America. It's an honor to meet you.''

The Chameleon blushes Crayola red and smiles. ''Thank you.'' His voice is a whisper, as if he's afraid to speak too loudly.

This is your teammate, the one who's going to help rescue Robin? You wonder what kind of trouble he helped ACT with in South America. This guy looks as if he'd run if you looked at him cross-eyed.

''Now,'' the Chief says, ''your first task when you arrive in Solonia will be to trace that telephone number. We've tried checking with Information over there and they insist that the number doesn't exist.''

You hate to do it, but you've got to tell them about the phone number. Even if it makes Robin look bad. ''Uh, Tracer, you know it's real hard for me to remember phone numbers. So I play a game where I turn the numbers into letters and see if they make a word.''

''I get the feeling you're leading up to something,'' Tracer says.

''I — I guess I am. The letters for that

telephone number in Solonia spell out BRUTE HEADQUARTERS.''

The Chief's face clouds up like an August thunderstorm. ''That is not good news.''

''Of course there are lots of other possible letter combinations. This might be just a coincidence!''

''Where BRUTE is concerned, there is no such thing as coincidence. I appreciate your telling us, Orion. It confirms my faith in your integrity. And doubles my doubts about and fears for your friend. BRUTE headquarters is not a healthy place to be, I suspect.''

You feel terrible, ratting on Robin, but your first allegiance is to ACT.

''So the chances of finding Robin alone and unguarded,'' the Chameleon says, ''are —''

''Slim to none,'' the Chief finishes for him. ''Which means we must have a believable tale to tell them if we need one. So'' — he pauses, his midnight gaze locked onto the Chameleon's face —''you, my friend, will pose as the mastermind and leader of a group of unprincipled teenage hackers.''

''Huh?'' you blurt.

''You have heard at one time or another of young people who've cut into various computer systems around the country. Chameleon's cover is that he has recruited a number of very bright teens who have computers, but no ethics. They, under his direction, have been systematically robbing banks by invading checking and saving accounts, transferring money electronically into an account that has been set up to receive stolen funds.''

''Ah,'' the Chameleon says, nodding. His eyes are gleaming with interest. You see now that they are blue and wonder why you didn't notice it before. ''And how does young Robin fit into this?'' he asks.

''A recent recruit,'' the Chief responds. ''And as one of your more knowledgeable hackers, you are not pleased to have had such a valuable resource snatched from your clutches. You feel strongly enough about this invasion into your territory to attempt a counter-kidnapping, as it were.''

''But Robin's going to deny it,'' you protest. ''He won't know what we've cooked up. He doesn't even know *me* by sight!''

''It will be your responsibility,'' the Chief replies, ''to give a clue as to your real identity. You may work that out for yourself. And as for Robin denying any involvement in the Chameleon's unsavory scheme, we will concoct for all of you, Robin included, very convincing criminal records.''

Tracer grins. ''Beautiful! A sting to sting a nest of hornets! Just the kind of thing they'd do themselves.''

The Chief returns his smile. ''I rather thought so. Chameleon, your cover name will be Jeffrey Cottwald the Third, born with money but too lazy to work to keep it.

You would rather use your considerable intelligence in other ways. You have been arrested innumerable times for fraud, but never convicted."

"Hmmm," the Chameleon says. You turn to look at him. Something about him seems different. His eyes are brighter, his features lean and firm instead of a mess of Silly Putty, and his posture is more erect. You blink and drop your gaze. *I'm going nuts*, you think.

"You, Orion," the Chief is saying, "will be Chris Mallory. We shall have to call upon our makeup experts to change your appearance, in the event that Oliver Gressom and Mr. Jones see you. Mr. Gressom might recognize you this time. And you will have a record as well."

He picks up two large envelopes from his desk and extends them to you and the Chameleon. "These contain detailed information on your identities. Study them carefully so you will be letter-perfect by the time you leave tonight."

"Then I'd better get to it," the Chameleon says, standing up. You can't help staring! He seems a foot taller now than when you first met him. And there's none of that "say 'boo' and I'll jump" look about him anymore. His chin is firm, his gaze direct. He smiles at you and it's a different smile from before, too. "See you later, pal," he says crisply and strides from the room.

"I'm sorry, Orion, but you should see your face," Tracer laughs.

"Uh, well, yeah," you stammer, wondering how to explain it. "I must be . . . It's just that he . . ."

The Chief roars with laughter. "Yes, I know what you mean! I reacted the same way the first time I saw the Chameleon do something like that."

You shake your head. "I don't get it. I can't even figure out what he did."

"He began to get into character," the Chief explains. "I think that's what the process is called. You see, the Chameleon is an actor."

"Boy, he sure is!" you agree. "But an actor, Chief? On a mission like this? After all, Robin's life is in danger!"

"There is still some question about that," the Chief responds. "There's no concrete evidence that Robin has been forced to go with them. Be that as it may, ACT is counting on Tracer's search-and-rescue talents, your knowledge of computers, and the acting abilities of one of the finest talents alive to save the neck of your errant friend."

You get up, your envelope under your arm. *Robin's a good kid,* you keep telling yourself. *Robin's a good kid.* He'd better be, because you are the one who insisted that ACT try to rescue him. And now it turns out you'll be sending a team into a nest full of BRUTEs!

CHAPTER 8

You began to have second thoughts about going on this mission when you saw how much stuff you'd have to memorize to be this Chris Mallory. Even more doubts crept up when they stuck your head in a vat of dye, bleached your eyebrows, and dabbed freckles all over your nose and cheeks. Now one glance at the crate that is supposed to fly you across the Atlantic to Solonia and you're ready to back out of the whole deal. The plane must be at least 25 years old and looks as if it's held together by rubber bands.

"Where's the Chameleon?" you ask Tracer as you buckle up your seatbelts. He wasn't in the car that brought you to the airport.

"His name's Jeffrey now," Tracer reminds you. "You'd better get used to calling him that because he won't answer to anything else. The Chief kept him for a last-minute briefing. He'll be here. Just cool it, Ori — I mean, Chris. Everything will work out fine."

Easy for him to say. He's a search-and-rescue man and that's what he's going to Solonia to do. The Chameleon's an actor and that's what he'll be doing. But your thing is computers, not pretending to be someone else. What if you get caught and BRUTE starts grilling you? What if you forget what your mother's first name is supposed to be or something dumb like that?

You sit and then glance warily around the cabin of the plane. At least the inside looks okay. The flight attendants wear costumes rather than uniforms — wide green skirts with bib aprons and white blouses with big puffy sleeves. They're blonde, rosy-cheeked, and pretty, with wide, friendly smiles. Perhaps too friendly, considering the wolfish grin of the tall man making his way to the seat across the aisle. He slips his briefcase under the seat in front of him and you notice the initials engraved under the handle: J.C.

Your mouth drops open as you look at him closely. "Tracer! That's —"

Tracer elbows you so hard, he knocks the wind out of you. "You're supposed to know him, remember?" he hisses, his teeth clenched.

"But — but . . ." You decide to shut up before you make an idiot of yourself. You would never have recognized the Chameleon. He seems taller, his hair is darker, and a stylist has been working at it. He has a Florida tan and his shoulders are broader. He looks very smooth, polished, and rich. Everything he wears has a symbol or some designer's initials on it.

He glances in your direction and waves a lazy, manicured hand in salute. "Hi. Just made it. Had a hard time finding a place to park the Rolls. Everything okay?"

You nod dumbly. Boy, when the Chief said the Chameleon was one of the finest actors alive, he wasn't kidding! He *is* Jeffrey Cottwald the Third! You dig into your book bag under the seat and get out your "Chris Mallory" notes. The Chameleon has shown you that there's a lot more to being a character than changing the color of your hair.

About an hour of it is all you manage before the activity of the day before and being up all night knock you out. You don't know how long you've been asleep when you become aware of Tracer talking to someone in tense tones. "Are you sure?" he's asking.

One of the flight attendants is bending over to speak to him. "Yes, sir, I'm sure." She smiles at you, her face bright with interest, and leaves.

"What's up?" you ask, yawning and rubbing your eyes.

"The pilot received a message for you from HQ."

"For me?"

"You're Chris Mallory, aren't you?" he says tersely. "The Chief wants you to turn on your computer."

"My — what for?"

"No questions," he snaps. "Just do it. Your computer at home is still linked to ours at HQ, and we've got a couple of satellites ours can use for communication anywhere in the world. So the Chief may be passing along something from your computer or sending a message of his own."

"Okay." The computer is in your book bag.

"No!" Tracer stops you. "Not out in the open. Take your bag back to the bathroom. I didn't see any suspicious faces, but you never can tell."

"Okay." Back in the restroom, there's barely space enough to turn around. Digging out your little portable unit, you power up, expecting instructions from ACT. Immediately, a garbled message begins to fill the monitor instead. That's Robin's code! What a relief to know that he's okay and trying to get in touch with you.

The message is short. Once it has ended and you've put it in memory, you type in the program to decode it. As the decoded words are spelled out, you begin to feel goosebumps rising all over your body. Robin's message reads:

TUCK! DANGER!! OVERHEARD A BOMB ABOARD SUNDAY FLIGHT TO SOLONIA!! ALERT AIRPORT OR POLICE OR SOMEBODY!! WILL BE IN TOUCH AGAIN. ROBIN.

You come out of that bathroom as if you were launched from a rocket.

"What is it?" Tracer asks softly. The Chameleon just watches, saying nothing.

"It was a message from Robin. There's a bomb aboard the plane."

"What?" Tracer is as pale as chalk. "Tell me precisely what it said. Quietly. We don't want to start a panic."

You repeat the warning, having no trouble remembering it. "What should we do?"

"Alert the pilot." Then he squints at you. "Any possibility that this is just a false alarm to flush us out, identify us as ACT agents?"

"Of course not!" you protest. "Robin doesn't know we're on this plane! And even if he does, why would he warn us at all if he was on their side? Why warn anybody?"

Tracer doesn't seem convinced, but gets up anyway and heads for the cockpit. He speaks softly to an attendant who doesn't waste any time. She opens the door and ushers him into the pilot's cabin.

A few minutes later, Tracer comes out of the cockpit, followed by a pink-cheeked young man in uniform. "The flight attendants are going to start looking for the thing. Sit tight."

"Anything I can do?" the Chameleon asks.

"Know any good prayers?" Tracer replies and follows the co-pilot toward the rear.

When the co-pilot comes back, he beckons to you. "The gentleman wants you," he murmurs softly.

"Me?" you squeak.

"Yes. Hurry, please." His face is wet with perspiration.

You trail him back to the bathroom where Tracer is waiting for you, squeezed into a corner. An open briefcase is perched on the sink.

"That's it," he says. "It was stashed under a case of napkins in the kitchenette."

You aren't sure what you're looking at; inside is a snarl of wires, something that resembles a digital clock, except that it doesn't show the time. You see a blob of pink stuff that looks like bubble gum.

"That's the explosive," Tracer says. "But look at that." He points to a small black gadget in the lid of the case.

You look at it. "It — it looks like a microcomputer, doesn't it?"

"I thought so, but I wasn't sure. That's why I called you."

You poke at it gingerly, trying not to move the wires connected to it. "It's a microcomputer set to trigger the bomb. But I don't know what that clocklike thing is. It says three-one-zero-zero-zero."

The co-pilot has his head in the door. "Hey, that's our altitude. We're at 31,000 and descending."

"My guess is that the thing is set to go off at a certain altitude," Tracer says. "What do you think? Can you do anything with it?"

Now it's your turn to sweat. "I don't know. I'll see."

Tracer moves into the corridor to give you more room.

You ask for a listing of the resident program to find out what altitude will set the bomb off. "Sixteen thousand feet," you say to the co-pilot. "Climbing *to* 16,000 was okay; it's coming down that will trigger it." You stare at him in panic. "Did you just say we're at 31,000 and descending? We can't descend or . . ."

"But we've got to!" the co-pilot insists. "We've got to stop and refuel in London. If we don't, we'll run out long before we get to Solonia."

"What if we just tossed the thing out of the plane?" Tracer asks.

"We can't do that either," you tell him. "It's set so that if it senses a drop in air pressure, it will blow immediately."

"In other words, we're sunk," Tracer says softly.

"Maybe not," you say, turning back to the computer. "There must be something that I can do."

Type the following program into your computer and run it. (Line 230 should be typed as one line on your computer.) Take a guess at the deactivation code. When you run the program, you can see that the plane is headed for real disaster! Quick — you've got to find some way to deactivate the bomb. List the program and study it carefully.

PROGRAM 5

```
 10 REM AIRBOMB
 20 HOME
 30 T$ = "            "
 40 REM THERE ARE 12 SPACES IN T$
 50 PRINT "DETONATION AT 16000 FEET"
 60 PRINT
 70 PRINT "DEACTIVATION CODE?"
 80 INPUT S$
 90 IF S$ = "BRUTE" THEN 100
100 PRINT T$;"ALTITUDE !"
110 PRINT T$;"---------- V"
120 PRINT
130 FOR I = 1 TO 15
140 FOR J = 1 TO I
150 PRINT "  ";
160 NEXT J
170 FOR K = 1 TO 500: NEXT K
180 PRINT "*";
190 FOR L = 1 TO 18 - I
200 PRINT "  ";: NEXT L
210 PRINT (32000 - 1000 * I);"  FT"
```

```
220 NEXT I
230 PRINT "==========
    =========+=== 16000 FT"
240 PRINT "BOOM!!"
250 END
260 PRINT "——————————————————"
270 PRINT "BOMB DEACTIVATED."
280 PRINT "——————————————————"
290 END
```

IBM	Apple		Radio Shack		Commodore		TI	Atari
PC & PCjr	II+	IIe	TRS-80	Color	64	VIC-20	99/4A	400/800
	✓	✓						

This program will run on the Apple II+ and Apple IIe. For all other computers, see the Reference Manual, page 121, for changes.

Checking through the complete listing this time, you pick up something new. "Hey! There's a deactivation statement in it."

"Hallelujah," Tracer says. "Use it!"

As your eyes scan the program, your spirits begin to sag again. "It wouldn't do any good. You have to use a certain word or phrase to send it into the deactivation statement, and I'm not sure what that is. But even if I figured it out, it still wouldn't work because of a mistake in the programming. See, when you enter the right word, it should send the bomb to the deactivation phase down here in this part of the program."

"Can you correct it?" Tracer asks.

"I think so. How much time do I have?"

The co-pilot answers, "Four, maybe five minutes. I'll see if we can get permission from Ground Control to stay up here a little longer." He quickly leaves for the cockpit.

You can't afford to wait for his answer. Tracer must agree, because you see him sneak a peek at his watch. He clears his throat but says nothing. He's leaving it up to you. So, cautiously, you begin.

The co-pilot reappears. "Five minutes at the most," he says, his voice cracking. "Then we *have* to start down."

"I've done everything I can," you tell him. "I just hope it works."

Tracer nods. "Go for it, Ace."

Nodding, you run the program.

Find the secret word that deactivates the bomb. Then fix the bug in the program so that the deactivation statement will work. If you need help, see the Reference Manual on page 122. Now run the program.

Tracer smiles. "Teammate, you did it again. Now, come on out of that bathroom. I need to use it — bad!"

CHAPTER 9

The refueling in London goes without a hitch. But your mind is busy with what might have been.

"Why do you think BRUTE wanted to blow up the plane?" you ask Tracer. "Do you think BRUTE knows we're on this plane? Does that mean they'll be waiting for us at Solonia?"

"I can't be sure. But ACT intelligence seems to think the bomb wasn't meant for us. They believe our cover is still good. Maybe BRUTE just wanted to keep outsiders out of Solonia until they can pull off their scheme."

"Well, bombing a plane would certainly discourage me from making Solonia my next vacation spot," you tell Tracer. But you're still not convinced the bomb wasn't meant for you. You'll find out soon enough, for there below you is Solonia.

From the air, it looks like a lot of toy villages spread out across a model railroad layout. Up close on the ground, it's like something on a calendar — tiny chalets perched on the sides of mountains, crisp green patches of lawn. And the people all look like the flight attendants on the plane — blond, rosy-cheeked, and plump. The women wear the wide, frilly skirts and puffy-sleeved blouses. The men wear those leather Bermuda shorts, long socks, and alpine hats.

Tracer could now pass for a Solonian. He had disappeared into a restroom at the airport and when he came out, he, too, was wearing shorts. Since the Chameleon just looked at him, smiled, and said nothing, you figure you'll keep your mouth shut, too. But he sure looks funny.

"Solonia's kind of pretty," you offer, as the three of you wait for a taxi.

"Pretty and poor," Tracer comes back, peering up the street. "Well, not really poor, just in deep financial trouble. Their treasury's almost bankrupt. They don't have anything to export and almost no tourist industry."

"There was practically nobody in the airport," you say.

"Isn't this a monarchy?" the Chameleon asks.

"There's a king, yes, but he's more a figurehead than anything else. Wonder what they do for cabs here?"

"You are American?" a little old man with a handcart asks. "You wish a taxi? I find one who speaks the English. A minute, please." He puts two fingers in his mouth and gives a whistle that would bring all the cabs in New York to a halt. From around the side of the terminal comes a bright-green horse-drawn cart. "Good, good," the old man says as it stops in front of you.

Tracer grins. "This is a taxi, huh? Thank you. To the Telephone Communications Building, please."

As the cart moves leisurely through the streets of this pretty little town, similar carts are all you see. "They don't have any cars?" you whisper to Tracer.

The driver has heard. "We have give them up, sir. We could no longer afford the petrol. Our merchants, they still use trucks, but the rest of us, we make do with carts such as these."

The cart has traveled several blocks before the green and white signs posted in every store window and on every tree make an impression on you. Passing a small coffeehouse, you lean out to take a closer look at it, which does no good since it's in Solonian. "Sir," you address the driver, "what do those signs say?"

"That? It urges our people to buy lottery tickets. They will draw the winner tomorrow."

The three of you look at one another. You've come just in time.

The Telephone Building is two stories and takes up a whole block. Inside, Tracer speaks to the Director of the Solonian Communications Commission. Whatever he tells him convinces the man to help you. He leads the three of you down to a basement room where one wall is completely covered by a giant map of the country. Colored lines crisscross it.

"This is our telephone system," the director explains. "Each colored line represents a particular exchange, which in Solonia is five numbers. You are trying to trace the source of a particular number?"

Tracer gives it to him. He goes to the map, where he points to the northwest corner. "The 27883 exchange would be in this quadrant of the country and, coincidentally, a part of this city. I have pulled out the directory where all numbers are listed — what is the word? — consecutively." He looks very pleased with himself. "So let's see."

He flips through several pages. "This exchange has the fewest listings of any, so it shouldn't take long to . . . ah, here we are." Frowning, he shakes his head. "No, we aren't. I'm sorry, sir, that number does not exist. Your number is 4323-7827-8377? The last two digits we have are 76. There is no 77."

The Chameleon, standing behind the director, looks over the man's shoulder at the directory. "Can you tell us who has the phone number that ends with 76?"

"Certainly." His long fingers trail across the page and his face lights up. "Of course! I should have been able to tell you that without looking. That's the telephone number to the country's one and only computer. We're very proud of it. It's used for the national lottery."

"The lottery?" you croak.

"Yes, indeed. See? The office telephone is 75 and 76 is the computer. We're hoping to enlarge our treasury a good deal with this lottery. If we don't . . ." A cloud crosses his face. "It is too disheartening to consider."

You wonder if they have Robin stashed at the lottery office. Suddenly, a high, piping sound splits the air.

"What is that?" the director asks.

"Uh — " You glance at Tracer in surprise. It's your micro.

"His travel alarm clock," the Chameleon says hurriedly. "You forget to cancel the alarm?" he asks.

"Uh — I sure did. Sorry." This calls for fast thinking. "Sir, is there a restroom I can use?" is the best you can do.

"Of course. Out that door, turn left."

"We'll wait for you here," Tracer says pointedly.

You hurry out, dart inside, and lock the door. Pulling out your unit, you push the Receive button. Robin's code flashes across the screen. Hoping you can get it decoded before someone comes in, you key in the program. Robin's message appears: FRIAR TUCK. HOPE YOU RECEIVE THIS. NEED HELP TO GET AWAY FROM THESE TERRIBLE MEN BUT DON'T KNOW WHERE I AM. LOTS OF BIG DOGS BARKING CLOSE BY. THEY SOUND AWFULLY WILD. STILL NOT SURE WHAT THESE PEOPLE WANT ME FOR. ROBIN. P.S. HOPE YOU STOPPED THE BOMB.

Powering down, you hurry back to Tracer and the Chameleon, your mind spinning. Lots of dogs nearby. A kennel? For wild dogs? That doesn't make sense. Unless the kennel is near the lottery office. For some reason, you're sure that's where they're keeping him.

"You must visit our cathedral," the director is saying, "and the museum, of course."

"We'll certainly try," Tracer says, edging away from him.

"And the National Solonian Zoo. By all means, visit the zoo. We're very proud of it."

"I'm sure," Tracer responds, trying to back away, but the director has him cornered. Even the Chameleon seems concerned, shooting worried looks in your direction.

Robin's message churns in your mind. While Tracer struggles to end the conversation politely, you glance at the open phone book. Your eyes lock on the last two telephone numbers — the lottery office and the computer line. You scan the numbers above them and your eyes widen. A whole series of telephone numbers, beginning with 8360 and going up to 8374, are all listed at the Solonian National Zoo!

"Excuse me, sir," you interrupt the director's commercial for Solonia, "but is the lottery office near the zoo?"

He stops and stares at you. "Why, yes, it is. Right across the street, to be exact."

You arrange a polite smile, somehow managing to hide your excitement. "Thank you, sir. We'd better be going now."

"Yes, we'd better," the Chameleon says smoothly. "We appreciate your help," he tells the director, grabbing Tracer's arm and leading him toward the door.

"Enjoy your stay in Solonia," the man calls. "And tell your friends to come visit."

"Thanks," Tracer says, once you're back out on the street. "I thought we'd never get away from him. What's happening, Chris?"

You're nearly hopping with excitement. "It was Robin again. He doesn't know where he is, but he says there are a lot of dogs barking close by. In the directory, all the phone numbers before the lottery office number are at the Solonian Zoo. That's where they must have him. He can probably hear animals from the zoo."

"It's worth a try," Tracer says. "Let's go."

But one look at the lottery office and it's plain that you couldn't hide a peanut butter sandwich in the building. It's a single-story structure with only one big room inside. No stairs, so that rules out a basement. Tracer cases the outside, just to be sure. The Chameleon offers to see what he can find out about the interior, pasting a smile on his face and sailing through the front door. When he comes out, the smile is gone. "Not in there," he grumbles. "I told them I was an architect and was interested in the design of the building. They showed me every nook and cranny, *and* their blessed computer. Our Robin is not in there."

"Then he must be in the zoo," you tell them, "somewhere near some dogs."

"Only one way to find out," Tracer mutters, looking across the street to the entrance to the zoo. "Let's go."

Inside the gates, each team member gets a copy of the zoo map. Tracer scans his quickly. "They don't have any dogs."

"Wolves, maybe?" you suggest.

"Wolves they've got," the Chameleon responds bitterly.

Checking the diagram, you begin to understand how he feels. The zoo seems to specialize in wolves. It has six different varieties, all in different sections of the park! This place is enormous. At this rate, you'll *never* find Robin!

CHAPTER 10

"The only sensible thing to do is split up," the Chameleon says crisply. "I'll take these two wolf bins, or whatever you call them. Tracer, how about you taking these two and, Chris, you check out the two over on this side." Somehow, he's assumed the mantle of leadership, which he seems to wear well. A sideways peek at Tracer shows that he doesn't seem to mind.

"Yes, sir," he says. "But remember, I'll have to act as if I'm not with you two. If that bomb was meant for us, they're bound to know we're still alive. And they'll be looking for three Americans."

The light dawns. "Oh! *That's* why you're wearing those short pants." You try not to laugh at his bony knees.

"They're called lederhosen, smartie, and I'm not wearing them to show off my legs!"

"Let's get to it," the Chameleon says.

"Wait a minute. What should we be looking for?" you ask.

The Chameleon has sense enough to let Tracer answer this one. "Any sort of enclosure around the wolf pens where a person could be hidden. If you see something that fits the bill, use your communicators and let us know."

"Roger," the Chameleon says smartly, turning on his heel and starting up the hill. Tracer grins after him and starts off in the other direction. Checking the map to get your bearings, you head left. When you look back, neither of your teammates is in sight.

Getting your bearings, you go on past the Siberian antelopes and some deer, around the monkey house and the building with the big cats, to the path that leads to the wolf compound. You know it's close because you can hear them barking and baying. Then there they are below, in a crater gouged out of the earth, the meanest-looking beasts you've ever seen.

And boy, are they big — almost the size of Great Danes. Their teeth look like mountain peaks. One of them stares up at you and drools. It makes you so edgy, you have to look away.

No simple fences for these guys; a rough stone wall arcs around in a semicircle. The crater itself is perhaps 10 feet below you. At the rear of the enclosed space is a big stone mound, the top of which is just about at eye level. The face of it is craggy with many openings that appear to be the mouths of caves. One of the beasts gets a running start and scrambles up the rugged ridges of the hill and disappears into one of the caves.

You try to gauge the depth of the caves, but there is a fence that keeps anyone from going beyond the point where the rock wall ends and the mound begins. Your eyes narrow, trying to see into the caves, but they are too far away.

"Tracer! Jeff!" you whisper into your communicator. "I may have found it! Up past the big cats."

"Be right there," Tracer replies.

"Right-o," the Chameleon echoes.

While you are waiting for your teammates to arrive, something happens that leaves no doubt you're in the right place. From somewhere at the top of the mound, a big man in a zoo uniform appears, carrying a large crate. He moves to the edge overlooking the crater and throws large chunks of raw meat down into the enclosure. The wolves rip into it, snarling, growling, fighting with one another. They are ferocious, and the thought of Robin being anywhere near them makes you feel a little sick. But the sight of the wolfkeeper makes you feel even worse. It's Oliver Gressom, in the flesh! Boy, are you grateful for that smelly dye they used on your hair!

Tracer lopes up, out of breath, his eyes glued to the scene below and the caves directly across. He stands some distance away. "Think you're right, Chris," he says out of the corner of his mouth.

"I *know* I am," you whisper. "Look at the man feeding the wolves."

Tracer's face tightens with anger. "Gressom! And they stashed that kid in there? With those — those man-eaters?"

The Chameleon is jogging up the hill. He slows as he approaches and watches the feeding with horrified fascination. "You aren't telling me that they're using *this* awful place as a prison? Why, those dirty . . . We've got to get Robin out of there immediately!"

You agree, but the wolves have begun to nibble at your courage. "Uh — Tracer, don't you think we should make sure Robin's in there before we make any plans?"

He moves farther away and turns his back.

"Oh, we will, we will," he says as softly as he can. "There must be someplace in there the wolves can't get to." He lifts the camera case he's carrying. "As soon as there's no one around and that gorilla's finished feeding those monsters, I'll take some readings."

"What kind?" the Chameleon asks, his face still flushed with anger.

The last visitor is moving away. Tracer opens the case and takes out a camera — except that it has what looks like a little TV screen on top of it. "This gizmo will make sonograms of the interior of the mountain, sort of like X rays, only they're made using sound waves. Then I can correlate the readings so we can pinpoint the most likely place Robin is stashed." He aims it as if he's going to take a picture.

"How long will all that take?" you ask.

"Not so loud," he warns you, stepping even farther away. "Getting the readings is the easy part. It's coordinating the readings to come up with how many meters in and how far up Robin is that will take the most time. I'm kind of slow with that kind of figuring."

"I'll do it on the computer," you volunteer.

A sheepish expression crosses Tracer's face. "Why didn't I think of that? Terrific! And if you act like a nosy kid trying to see what I'm doing, maybe you can take down the readings for me. Think you can do that?"

That rates a grin. "Sure."

"Good. Gressom's gone. Let's get to work before someone else comes." He takes out the mechanism and, pointing the lens at the rocky enclosure, begins to walk slowly from the left side back toward the center. You trail him, trying to act like a nuisance without really getting in his way. When a likely space inside the mound shows up on the viewing screen, he calls out the readings to you. "I've got 33, 24,

13, 10, then 22. Okay? Now, 52, 17, 34, 18, 35. That's from the south wall."

"Got it," you respond.

He goes around toward the right side. "Okay, now — 66, 77, 88, 98, 97. Okay? Now, 54, 85, 67, 33, 29. That's the east side," he calls.

"Got it," you answer. Now to key in a program that will make sense of all that. If anyone notices what you're doing, you hope they'll think it's a portable computer game.

Type the following program into your computer. Note: There are 20 equal signs between the quotes in lines 240 and 370. Lines 240 and 370 must each be typed as one line on your computer. Run the program and then put in the readings Tracer gave you when the computer asks for the X and Y readings. The X readings are the ones taken along the south wall. The Y readings are the ones from the east.

PROGRAM 6

```
10 REM SONOGRAM
20 X = 0
30 Y = 0
40 FOR J = 1 TO 10
50 PRINT "ENTER X READING ";J;
60 INPUT X1
70 IF X1 <= X THEN 100
```

```
80 N = J
90 X = X1
100 NEXT J
110 PRINT
120 FOR J = 1 TO 10
130 PRINT "ENTER Y READING ";J;
140 INPUT Y1
150 IF Y1 <= Y THEN 180
160 P = J
170 Y = Y1
180 NEXT J
190 PRINT
200 PRINT "ROBIN'S LOCATION:"
210 PRINT "WEST WALL: ";N;" METERS"
220 PRINT "NORTH WALL:";P;" METERS"
230 PRINT
240 PRINT
    "========================"
250 PRINT ;
260 FOR I = 1 TO 10
270 FOR J = 1 TO 10
280 IF P <> I THEN 320
290 IF N <> J THEN 320
300 PRINT "**";
310 GOTO 330
320 PRINT "..";
330 NEXT J
340 PRINT
360 NEXT I
370 PRINT
"========================"
380 END
```

IBM	Apple		Radio Shack		Commodore		TI	Atari
PC & PCjr	II+	IIe	TRS-80	Color	64	VIC-20	99/4A	400/800
✓	✓	✓	✓	✓	✓	✓	✓	✓

The program will run on all the computers checked off on this chart.

"Good work, Orion," Tracer says as Robin's location appears on your monitor. "Now we have to get in there. There must be a way from on top or behind the mound."

You check the map. "The reptile house is back there. Maybe we can see it from there."

"It's worth a try," the Chameleon says.

The situation looks good. Standing with your back to the reptile house, you can look right across at a door in the back of the mound. A wire fence runs along the walkway, but you should be able to climb over it.

Tracer ambles past the Chameleon and stops, as if trying to decide whether to go in and see the snakes. "That's no cheap lock, but I think I can pick it." He turns to look at the two of you. "So, we go in tonight?"

On the far side of the mound, the wolves are still growling. The sound makes you queasy. Then you think of how it must sound to Robin, and nod. "We go in tonight."

CHAPTER 11

Sneaking through the zoo at night is like going through a House of Horrors. Everything looks different. The shadows are black, bottomless. You feel that if you step into the darkness, you'll never be seen again.

The animals stir in their cages and pens, grumbling and growling, but because you can't see them clearly, they seem more threatening. Tracer strides past them without even glancing in their direction. The Chameleon has to hurry to keep up; you have to run.

The reptile house is up ahead. Tracer stops, finger to his lips, and pulls the two of you off the path into the darkness. "We'll have to keep under the trees now, in case someone's on watch. Stay behind me."

A super idea. An even better one would be to catch the next plane home. Tracer leads the way up the incline, and stops beside the reptile house. The concrete snakes next to the doors seem to writhe in the eerie yellow light cast by the lamps along the walkway.

"Wait here," Tracer whispers and disappears into the gloom. The night drops down around you, heavy and full of weird sounds.

"Scared?" the Chameleon asks quietly. A nod is all you can manage. "Me, too," he says, and squeezes your shoulder. Suddenly, you realize that you like him a lot.

There is a rustling ahead. You freeze, hear the Chameleon's indrawn breath. Tracer appears, a solid shape emerging from the inky darkness. "That lock was a cinch. Either we're wrong and there's nobody in there, or those guys are awfully sure of themselves. Are you sure I can't convince you to take a gun?"

"So I can shoot myself in the foot? No, thanks, I'll manage without it," the Chameleon answers.

Tracer shrugs, giving up. "Okay. Ready?"

"Ready," you croak.

"Ready," the Chameleon echoes.

The short walk to the door in the mound feels like the last few steps to the gallows. Before Tracer opens the door, he whispers, "Remember the signal. One beep if you're able to come back out this way; two if you'll need to go through the front. I'll be waiting for you either way."

Your stomach quivers its way down around your ankles. The "front," as he calls it, means going right through the wolf pen — not under it! Even at this hour, the wolves are not asleep. You can hear them snarling, growling. The thought of trying to escape past those drooling monsters sends a parade of wormy sensations down your spine. A glance at the Chameleon, however, makes you feel a little better about yourself. He looks as if he's about to be sick.

"Well, let's get on with it," Tracer whispers, easing the door open and peeking inside. "All clear. Go!"

The Chameleon squares his shoulders, gives you a wink, and slips into the entrance of the hill. You're right behind him, sticking to him like glue — until you feel the floor shake under your feet. You're on a catwalk. It's suspended a good 20 feet above the floor, and the only thing between you and disaster is the narrow path and two skinny handrails. You freeze, your eyes fixed on the pit below. The Chameleon is 15 feet ahead before he realizes he's by himself.

Looking back, he hesitates, then retraces his steps. He grabs your hand. "Keep it on my shoulder," he whispers, "and don't look down. Look at the back of my head, look at the ceiling — just don't look down. I'll lead, you follow, okay?"

The Chameleon turns and sets off again. Your hand is locked onto his shoulder, your eyes burn into the back of his neck. He walks left, then right, and stops. "Need some help here," he whispers. "Which door?"

Scraping at the edges of your courage, you take a look around. The interior of the mound is a tic-tac-toe grid of iron beams. Some of the spaces between the beams are enclosed, and you realize you're looking at the outside walls of the wolves' caves. There are two on the level above you, three on this one, and two on the one below. Each has a door.

Tracer has briefed you about the general direction to go — to the right on this level. But there are two doors on this side and it looks as if one leads right into wolf country.

Closing your eyes, you picture yourself out "front." Seven meters from the west wall, two from the north. With a deep breath, you point to the door on the extreme right.

"You're sure?" the Chameleon asks.

"Pretty sure."

He gazes at you for a long, long moment and smiles. "Then what are we waiting for?" Striding to the fateful door, he turns the knob. It does not give. He takes a long, thin instrument from his pocket, glares at the lock, and puts the instrument into the keyhole. A few wiggles of the thing and there's a click so soft you can barely hear it. He glances back at you in triumph, and tries the knob again. The door opens noiselessly.

The Chameleon takes one, two, three deep breaths, and grins. "Show time," he whispers, and in one rapid movement, darts through the door — and almost runs smack into a second closed door. He stops short and tries the knob of this one, which turns easily in his hand. He pulls open the door — and nearly runs smack into Gressom!

"Out of my way, caveman," the Chameleon snarls. "I'm here to get my property!"

True to form, Gressom reaches into the jacket of his uniform and pulls out the huge black cannon of a gun that he had pointed at you in the shopping center. "Hey! Who are you?" he rasps. "How'd you get in here?"

The Chameleon plants his palm against Gressom's chest and shoves. Gressom stumbles backward. "I repeat," the Chameleon says, "I'm here to get my property. Robin!"

"Huh?" a small, frightened voice calls.

Edging your way past the Chameleon and around Gressom, you come to a dead halt. Robin's there all right, sitting on a folding chair in a far corner next to a row of terminals, hands and feet tied. It's a contest between the two of you as to which of you is more surprised. You figure you would win. Robin is a girl!

At the moment, she's all eyes — big, soft, dark, almond-shaped under a fringe of mahogany bangs. A ponytail bounces from the top of her head and flops over one shoulder. She looks like a scared 12-year-old.

"Hands up," Gressom growls.

The Chameleon curls his lip with disgust. "Don't be stupid. You plan to shoot someone in a room with metal walls and have bullets ricocheting all over the place? Now put that thing away and stop wasting my time. I want the girl."

"If it was up to me, you could have the brat," Gressom snaps as he lowers the gun. "She's more trouble than she's worth. And she kicks. Look at my shins!" He pulls his pant-leg up to show the black-and-blue marks.

While the Chameleon keeps Gressom occupied, you move quickly to Robin's side and begin to untie her. "Friar Tuck to the rescue," you whisper, pushing aside the tray of food on the floor. She hadn't eaten much.

Her eyes begin to sparkle. "It *is* you! You got my messages!"

"You bet. Shhhh! Just go along with whatever we say, understand?"

"Gotcha," she grins. You really like this kid. She's got guts.

As you struggle with the ropes, you can feel a sudden change in the atmosphere. Robin has tensed, the Chameleon has broken off in the middle of a sentence. You look up. Standing in the doorway is a skeleton, a tall, bone-thin man, his head as hairless as a Ping-Pong ball. But the face is what makes the biggest impression. It's a death's head — dark, sunken eyes above cheekbones so sharp you could cut yourself on them. His entrance brings a silence as thick as pea soup.

"Oliver." His voice is a hollow whisper. "You should have let me know we had guests." He directs a piercing gaze toward the Chameleon, then at you. You can feel a cold sweat on your forehead. "I am Dr. Nicholas Arsene. And you, sir?"

The Chameleon turns his back on Gressom. "Jeffrey Cottwald the Third, Dr. Arsene. My pleasure. And my young assistant, Chris Mallory. I am here to convince this double-crossing little member of my team of the error of her ways and to take her home. Really, Robin," he adds mournfully, "I'm disappointed in you."

Robin, to her credit, makes a sulky face.

"Your mission intrigues me," Dr. Arsene replies as he comes in and shuts the door. "A member of your team, you say?"

The Chameleon hesitates, his eyes measuring Dr. Arsene. "Well, I suppose it's safe to tell *you,*" he says finally. "Robin's one of a group of young recruits of mine — call them computer soldiers, if you like. There are any number of American banks that would swear to just how expert my crew is as they've watched deposits disappear from their computers."

"I see," Arsene murmurs. "Tapping into checking and savings accounts."

"That's just one phase of the operation." The Chameleon's voice is as smooth as an oil slick. "Then there are the credit card scams.

Unauthorized charges — that's how I got my Rolls. And those lovely automatic money machines that dispense cash, given the proper computerized code. It's penny-ante stuff, I admit, but it all adds up."

Dr. Arsene regards the Chameleon with distaste. "What a sad little fairy tale, Mr. Cottwald. Is that the best you could come up with to get in here? Do you expect me to believe that Robin takes part in such activities?"

"She latched onto your lottery scam, didn't she?" the Chameleon says.

Dr. Arsene focuses on Robin. "There is that, isn't there?"

"True, she did it without my knowledge, but that should prove she's no two-bit hacker," the Chameleon adds.

"And she's just a beginner." You jump in to take some of the load off the Chameleon. "Why do you think she got caught?"

"Big mouth," Robin snarls.

"I bet she pulled her sweet, innocent act for you, didn't she?" the Chameleon says with a laugh. "You should check that out with a couple of judges in Juvenile Court."

"That kid's got a record?" Gressom asks.

"All of my 'kids' have records," the Chameleon brags. "It's one way to keep some sort of control over them."

"Hey!" Robin yells. "That's an invasion of my privacy! And besides, a person's juvenile records are supposed to be hidden."

"They are," you tell her, smirking. "Hidden on computer."

She blinks. "Oh."

"And you, Mr. Cottwald," Dr. Arsene says. "What are your — qualifications?"

"If you're asking if I have a record," the Chameleon says coldly, "it's none of your business. Besides, they couldn't prove a thing and they tried, all six times."

There is a silent exchange between Dr. Arsene and Gressom, who nods and leaves.

"You understand that we *will* check on your tawdry little tale," Dr. Arsene says. "As for releasing Robin, I'm sorry, but we have our own plans for her."

"The Solonian lottery, huh?" you pipe up. "You want Robin to rig the results so that one of you wins the prize."

"Not just the prize money," Robin says loudly, "*all* the money the Solonians have paid for the lottery tickets."

"Which will wipe out their hopes of bailing their national treasury out of hock," the Chameleon purrs, his voice full of admiration, "and then this place is yours. Smooth."

"You know what else?" Robin howls. "They want me to do it for *nothing*! Can you beat that?" She's really getting into her part!

"You guys are going to own a whole country?" you ask. "Just who are you? Whoever you are, I'd like to be on your side."

"What?" The Chameleon spins around.

"Face it, Jeff," you tell him with a sneer, playing your role to the hilt. "Compared to this operation, the stuff you do is small time. I've got to look out for my future." You move closer to the walking skeleton. "Look, Dr. Arsene, Robin's good, but I'm better; I've been at it longer. There must be a place for me somewhere in your organization."

"Why, you — you . . ." the Chameleon sputters. "That's gratitude for you! I bailed you out of Juvenile Hall, took you in — "

"And used my brains to line your pockets. So we're even. How about it, Dr. A.?"

Gressom returns before Dr. Arsene can respond, and hands him three sheets of paper. The ice-cold eyes scan them quickly. "Jeffrey Cottwald: suspicion of fraud, grand larceny, embezzlement. Dismissed. Chris Mallory: petty larceny, extortion, breaking and entering. Robin Gold: petty larceny."

"It was a bum rap," Robin yells angrily. "I was framed!"

"How'd you get that?" the Chameleon demands.

"We have a system of satellites that allows us to cut in on any computer, radio, or television in the world," Dr. Arsene replies.

"Hot dog!" you chortle. "Come on, Dr. Arsene, let me work with you. I can be very useful. Let me prove it. Need a million dollars or so to tide you over for a little while?"

"A million dollars?"

''Sure. Which one of these terminals is connected to the outside world?''

''That one,'' Robin answers, pointing.

''Give me an hour without your trained gorilla looking over my shoulder,'' you urge, ''and I'll transfer a cool million into any account you have anywhere. That ought to prove I know my stuff. What do you say?''

Dr. Arsene considers the suggestion and glances again at the sheets in his hand. ''Very well. Consider this an audition. But I won't be so foolish as to give you an account number just yet. Set up an account for us here in the National Bank of Solonia and transfer the million into that. You have an hour.''

''Hey, what about me?'' the Chameleon asks. ''Any organization can always use another idea man.''

''It is obvious you have no idea of the size and nature of our organization,'' Arsene responds icily, ''or you would never have been so foolish as to break in here. As for using you, we'll see, we'll see. Come, Oliver. There can be no harm in leaving them here unguarded. They have no place to go.'' He turns to lead the way from the room.

''I'll be right outside,'' Gressom announces, ''so don't try anything funny.'' He glares one last time at Robin and leaves.

The Chameleon looks after him. ''Tracer was right. I should have taken the gun.''

CHAPTER 12

"This is all my fault," Robin says. "I never meant for anything bad to happen."

"Why'd you start messing with their lottery anyway?" you ask her.

"I didn't know it was theirs; I thought it was just a supermarket thing. I had been buying tickets, zapping the computer to make sure the ones I bought would win, and then I sent the tickets to people who needed the food or the money."

"Then why me? Did you think I needed the money?"

"No, but don't you remember? You told me about the computer class you teach at that neighborhood center. You said the center didn't have much money and they had only one computer. You said you wished there was a way for you to get more computers for the kids. So I fixed it so you could get them."

You blush with shame. Not once after you found out you had the winning ticket did you think about computers for the center.

"It was a very dangerous idea, Robin," the Chameleon offers kindly. "Now how about coming up with an idea that will get us out of here. That big ape outside sort of fouls things up for leaving from that direction."

"There's another way out," Robin says, "but we can't use it because there are dogs out there. They sound as if they bite."

"Eat you alive is more like it," you tell her. "They aren't dogs, they're wolves. But where is this other door?"

She goes to the terminal on the end and keys in a sequence. Suddenly the end wall begins to slide open. Beyond the door is darkness and the wolves! "That awful Gressom man showed me this last night, to prove to me I couldn't get away. After he left, I fooled around until I found out how to open it."

"Does it lead to one of the caves for the wolves?" the Chameleon asks, peering out.

"I don't know. It's a tunnel. I went down it a little way, but then I heard the wolves and came back."

"I'd better go see." The Chameleon disappears into the darkness.

"I want to thank you for coming," Robin says when he's gone. "I'm sorry I got you into this, but it's nice not being all alone."

"Well, if our luck holds," you tell her,

"we'll be out of this place in a flash. . . . I'd better get to work."

Robin looks horrified. "Are you really going to get that million dollars for them?"

"Of course not!"

"Good. They don't need it anyhow."

"How do you know?"

"Well, I didn't have anything else to do last night, so after Gressom left, I started playing around with the computer and I found one of their accounts. I don't know where it is, but it's got forty-six million dollars in it."

"Forty-six. . . . What's the account number? We're going to hit them where it hurts while we have the chance."

She looks delighted at the thought and rattles off the numbers you need.

"This shouldn't be too hard. First I'll withdraw half of BRUTE's money. Then I'll transfer that money to the ACT account. They set one up for me to 'borrow' the million dollars from. Then I'll just take the rest of BRUTE's money and transfer that to the Solonian lottery account. I think BRUTE owes them a little something."

"Super!" Robin cries. "That almost makes this whole thing worth it."

It's time to get back to business. You finger the medallion around your neck and press a tiny button on its back side twice.

"What's that?" she asks.

"A beeper. There's help waiting outside.

I was signaling him to let him know we'll have to go out the — the front way.''

''You mean, past the wolves?'' she asks.

''We've got no choice with Gressom outside the back door.''

''What are you going to do?''

''When we get out,'' you tell her, sounding more positive than you feel, ''we'll go to the airport. But we need some cover. That place is so empty, Gressom and his crew would be able to catch us in a minute. So I'm going to cut into computers the air traffic controllers use and divert all the flights within a thousand miles to Solonia's airport.'' BRUTE's communication system will be their own undoing!

Twenty-five minutes later, BRUTE is forty million dollars poorer and there are 11 planes headed toward Solonia's airport.

The Chameleon comes back looking worried. ''Doesn't look good,'' he says tersely. ''The tunnel slopes down and there's a very heavy grid at the end of it. Not even wire cutters would work on that thing. And I'm not sure, but I think there may be another one down the line. I could just barely see it.''

''That's right,'' Robin says. ''I remember now. Gressom said something about there being three of them. He told me they're electrically controlled, and anybody who touches them would be electrocuted.''

''That's not true,'' the Chameleon responds, ''because I touched it when I looked for a switch. There isn't one. I don't know how we're going to do it, but we'll have to overpower Gressom and go out the way we came.''

''We can't,'' you cry. ''I've already signaled Tracer we're coming out the other way.''

The Chameleon turns pale. ''Oh, boy.''

''I bet the computer controls the grids, too,'' Robin suggests.

''Only one way to find out,'' you mutter, moving over to the next terminal. You ask for a directory of programs and there it is.

Type the following program into your computer and run it. Line 100 has four spaces between quotes; line 110 has five spaces.

PROGRAM 7

```
 10 REM GRIDSUP
 20 HOME
 30 W = INT(38/5)
 40 N = 9
 50 A$ = "!!"
 60 B$ = "!!"
 70 C$ = "!"
 80 FOR I = 1 TO W
 90 A$ = A$ + "----!"
100 B$ = B$ + "    !"
110 C$ = C$ + "     "
120 NEXT I
130 A$ = A$ + "!"
140 B$ = B$ + "!"
```

```
150 C$ = C$ + " !"
160 GOSUB 270
170 GOSUB 320
180 GOSUB 270
190 FOR I = 1 TO 500
200 NEXT I
210 FOR I = 1 TO 20
220 PRINT C$
230 FOR J = 1 TO 100
240 NEXT J
250 NEXT I
260 END
270 FOR I = 1 TO N
280 PRINT A$
290 PRINT B$
300 NEXT I
310 RETURN
320 PRINT "ENTER THE ENTRY CODE";
330 INPUT Q$
340 IF Q$ <> "51" THEN 370
350 HOME
360 RETURN
370 PRINT "THE GRID IS SEALED"
380 END
```

IBM	Apple		Radio Shack		Commodore		TI	Atari
PC & PCjr	II+	IIe	TRS-80	Color	64	VIC-20	99/4A	400/800
	✓	✓						

The program will run on the Apple II+ and Apple IIe. For all other computers, see the Reference Manual, page 124, for changes.

"The program works on an entry code system," you say. "I may be able to break it."

Then you hear Gressom's voice outside the door. The Chameleon grabs a chair and jams it under the knob. "Hurry," he whispers.

It all comes down to this. If you don't get the entry code right, the grid will not open — and you, Robin, and the Chameleon will be at the mercy of Gressom and Arsene. "Well, here goes nothing . . ." you say.

Can you figure out what code to use to open the grid? Run the program and try it. If you need help, see page 126 of the Reference Manual.

"Yipeee!" Robin's cheer is music to your ears. But your moment of victory is brief. To your horror, the room is suddenly pitch black!

"Oh, no!" Robin's voice is hoarse with panic. "The electricity is out. It happened last night, too. Gressom got very upset and said that was one thing he hated about Solonia. I think he's afraid of the dark. Did you get to finish the program?"

"Just barely. I don't know if there was time for it to work before the power went off. And if these terminals don't have any kind of protection against power outages and the program crashed, we're up the creek."

The lights flicker and come back on. "Do I have time to put the program in again?" you ask the Chameleon.

His ear is glued to the door. "No way. The voices are coming closer. Look, you two start into the tunnel and we'll cross our fingers that the grids are up or at least partway up. This chair will delay Gressom for a few minutes. I've got a few smoke capsules with me. As soon as he gets the door open, I'll break them and that should give you another few minutes. Now, get out! I'll follow as soon as I can."

"But, Chameleon," you say, realizing your slip too late, but you're worried about him. He may end up sacrificing his life so that you and Robin can get away.

"Listen," he assures you, "I'll make it. Now scram!"

As precious as time is, you take a moment to do one more thing. Picking up a glass of water from Robin's tray, you pour it over the keyboard of BRUTE's super-computer. There are a series of sharp, crackling sounds. The keyboard begins to hiss and then shoot sparks. At last, the whole shebang spits out a great gust of smoke and the screen blacks out. "That'll fix 'em," you growl.

Grabbing Robin's hand, you sprint out to the tunnel. Nearing the first grid, Robin shouts, "It's up! It's up!"

The tunnel begins a sharp downward slope toward ground level. Somewhere outside the wolves have begun to bark excitedly.

Robin stops. ''I'm scared. Listen to them!''

''That's the sound I wanted to hear,'' you tell her. ''If I'm right, those monsters are very busy and won't pay one bit of attention to us. Now come on!'' You grab her arm and start to run again.

The second grid is only halfway up and you have to stoop to get under it. The third grid freezes your blood. It had just started up when the power went off. It's barely a foot from the ground.

''On your back!'' you shout. Pulling her down, you both wriggle your way under it and barely make it without ripping your clothes. If it's that tight for you, how will the Chameleon make it under?

You dart toward the sounds of snarling, gnashing teeth. At the mouth of the tunnel, you pause, pushing Robin behind you while you check to make sure things are going according to plan. Ten feet up on the walkway around the enclosure, Tracer waves to you. Then he takes two enormous chunks of meat, staggering under their weight, and tosses them into the compound. The wolves hurl themselves on the meat, snarling, ripping it to shreds as they eat. Tracer points to the right side of the compound where a rope ladder hangs.

"Over there," you pant. "Let's go!" You run for the ladder and hear the sound of Robin's feet behind you. "You first," you tell her, guiding her foot to the first rung. "Hurry!"

As she scrambles up, you turn back, running to the mouth of the tunnel again, hoping for some sign that the Chameleon is coming. Robin is halfway up the ladder and making good time. You wonder how much meat Tracer has left to unload. If he runs out before you and the Chameleon can start up the ladder. . . .

The sound of running feet takes your mind off the wolves and you duck back into the tunnel. The Chameleon is barreling toward the last grid. Seeing it, he stops.

"Come on," you urge him. "You can make it under!"

"Don't kid me, Orion. I'm too big!" His face shows his helplessness. He's given up.

Suddenly you have an idea. You call to the Chameleon.

"Okay, maybe Jeff Cottwald is too big, but . . . what if you were Dr. Arsene? I bet he could get under. Come on, get into it! You're Dr. Arsene."

"Oh, come on, Orion!"

"Try it! I've seen what you can do! Concentrate! You're Dr. Arsene!"

Before your eyes, the Chameleon begins to change. It's the creepiest thing you've ever seen. His face seems to be getting thinner. He seems to shrink inside his clothes. Dropping to the ground, he lies on his back and wriggles under the grid.

"Hot dog!" you yell as he gets to his feet. "You did it! Let's go."

But outside, your luck has run out because Tracer has run out of meat. Robin stands next to him, peering down in the compound.

The wolves have gotten your scent and are beginning to slink in your direction. They've just gobbled down a ton of meat, but you're sure they're *still* ready to eat you. Three of them, more bold than the others, turn in your direction. Are they planning to attack?

You take off toward the ladder, your heart pounding so hard it's making your whole body shake. The Chameleon, however, has stopped. He glares at the three wolves with Dr. Arsene's eyes, Dr. Arsene's deadly expression. "Get back!" he barks at them. "Get back over there! And stay there!" Like a miracle, they begin to retrace their steps and finally turn to skulk back to the others.

The Chameleon walks slowly to the ladder and follows you up. At the top, you turn and help him over the wall. Not until then does he drop the personality of Dr. Arsene.

"That was the most marvelous thing I've ever seen," Robin cries.

The Chameleon grins. "It was pretty good, wasn't it? Now can we get into the truck? I think I'm going to faint."

CHAPTER 13

You begin to laugh as soon as you push through the doors to the airport. The terminal lobby is in pure chaos, jammed with grumpy travelers. Outside, the runways look like an airplane parking lot.

The elderly porter who helped you get a cart-cab yesterday hurries by, grinning from ear to ear. "Is this not wonderful?" he asks, recognizing you. "No one knows how they came to be here but now that they are, we will make them feel welcome, make them want to stay and come back again. Perhaps they will tell others and the others will come. Ah, what it would do for our treasury!" He hurries away and you wonder what he would say if he knew that the treasury was twenty-three million dollars richer already!

"Uh — we'd better get going," the Chameleon mutters. "I think I see a fathead friend of ours."

You look back. Coming through the door, face red with fury, is Gressom. Behind him is Dr. Arsene, his burning eyes scanning the mob until he sees you. If looks could kill, the three of you would be pushing up daisies tomorrow. He starts in your direction, but there are too many people in his way; he knows he could never reach you in time. His expression is bitter, his shoulders droop in defeat.

"This way," Tracer says, as the four of you dart out of a door and sprint across several runways toward a helicopter.

On the way, a thought occurs to you. "Tracer." You keep your voice low. "You knew Robin was a girl, didn't you?"

A wicked grin lights his lean features. "Sure, we cased her house, remember?"

"How come you didn't tell me?" you ask.

The grin widens. "Pure meanness. It was nice knowing something you didn't."

As you climb into the helicopter, a sheet of paper, whipped by the wind, swoops and swirls across your paths and gets caught under Robin's heel. She stoops to pick it up, looks at it, and grins. It is one of those flyers advertising Solonia's lottery.

"Going to buy a ticket?" you ask.

Robin shakes her head quickly. "Never again as long as I live. Maybe I should try to pay back the supermarket people, but it'll take me the rest of my life. I don't get much of an allowance."

You fasten your seatbelt. "Robin, don't worry about that. Dr. Arsene and his gang *own* the supermarkets."

Robin's eyes go round in surprise. "They do?" She sits back in her seat and becomes very quiet. "Chris," she says finally, "I'm scared. They own the supermarket. They have — well, they *had* forty-six million dollars in one account and Dr. Arsene said they have others. They have their own satellite. And they think nothing of cleaning out the treasury of a poor country and taking it over."

"So?" you ask, wondering where she's going with this.

"So, sure, I'm only a kid, but I've got sense enough to know that Dr. Arsene and Gressom and all the rest of them, they aren't your two-bit late-show gangsters. If they'd gotten away with taking over Solonia, the next thing you know, they would start thinking about taking over our country, or the whole world even. Who's going to stop them. Somebody's got to try!"

You settle in your seat and clamp your jaws closed. As much as you'd like to, you know you can't answer her question. If you could, you would tell her about ACT and about its fight to defeat BRUTE's plans for worldwide domination. You would answer her cry that someone must try to stop BRUTE by telling her not to worry — as long as ACT exists, somebody will be trying.

REFERENCE MANUAL

Note to User: The programming activities in this book have been designed for use with the BASIC programming language on the IBM PC, PCjr, Apple II Plus or Apple IIe (with Applesoft BASIC), Commodore 64, VIC-20, TI 99/4A, Atari 400/800, Radio Shack TRS-80 Level 2 or greater, and the Radio Shack Color Computer. Each machine has its own operating procedures for starting up BASIC. So make sure you're in BASIC before trying to run any of these programs.*

The version of the program included in the text will run on most of the computers listed above. However, a few of the commands used are not available on some home systems. If the program as given does not run on one of the

*Also make sure you type NEW before entering each program to clear out any leftovers from previous activities.

micros above, modification instructions will be included in this Reference Manual. TI 99/4A users, please note: The Texas Instruments version of regular BASIC doesn't allow multiple statements on a line or the word GOTO following a THEN. Multiple statements on the same line should be entered as one statement per line number and any THEN GOTO line number should be entered as just THEN line number.

Even if you're using a computer other than the ones mentioned, the programs may still work, since they are always written in the most general BASIC.

If you need help with one of the computer activities in the *Micro Adventure*, or want to understand how a program works, you'll find what you need in this manual.

Naturally, programs must be typed into your computer *exactly* as given. If the program should run on your computer but you're having problems, do a list on the program and check your typing before you try anything else. Even a misplaced comma or space might cause an error of syntax that will prevent the whole program from working.

TERMS YOU NEED TO KNOW

Computer experts have a special "language" they use when talking about programs. Here are some common terms that will help you understand the explanations in this manual.

Arrays are groups of two or more logically related data elements in a program that have the same name. However, so that the individual elements in the array can be used, each is also identified by its own address (called an *index* by programmers). You can think of an array as an apartment building. One hundred people might live at the Northwest Apartments (or 100 pieces of information might be stored in the NW Array). But each unit within the building has a number (like Apt 14), so that it can be located and receive mail. In the NW Array, 14 could be the index to find a particular piece of information, and would be written NW (14). If you put the 26 letters of the alphabet into an array called Alpha, then Alpha (2) would equal B because B is the second letter of the alphabet.

ASCII (pronounced *asskee*) is the standard code used by most microcomputers to represent characters such as letters, numbers, and punctuation.

ASC is a function in BASIC that will supply a character's ASCII code. For example ASC(''A'') will give you the number 65.

Bugs are errors or mistakes in a program that keep it from doing what it's supposed to do. Some of the programming activities in this book will ask you to find and fix a bug so that the program will work correctly.

Functions are ready-made routines that perform standard calculations in a program. It's sort of like having a key on a calculator that computes a square root or the cosine of a number. The programming language BASIC comes with a number of standard functions to perform certain tasks. For example, the function SQR (x) will find the square root of any number when x is replaced by that number. You might want to check the BASIC manual that came with your computer to see which functions are available on your system.

INT is a function that changes any number that you supply into a whole number or integer. For example INT(4.5) will return the value 4. For numbers greater than 0, INT just throws away any fractions and supplies you with the whole number.

Loops are sections of programs that may be repeated more than once—usually a specified number of times, or until certain conditions are met. For example, if you wanted to write a program that would count from 1 to 100, a loop could be used to keep adding 1 to a counter variable until the number 100 was reached. Loops are most commonly formed with FOR/NEXT statements or GOTO commands. You'll find many examples of these in the programs in this book.

Random Number Generator This function, which is called RND in BASIC, lets you generate numbers at ''random'' just as though you were throwing dice and didn't know which number was coming up next. In most home computers, the RND function returns a fraction between 0 and 1. To get numbers in a larger range, the program must multiply the fraction by a larger number. For example, RND * 10 will produce numbers between 0 and 10.

REM This command is used to tell the computer that whatever is on a particular line is just a comment or a remark and should not be executed. An example might look like this:

```
10 REM THIS PROGRAM COUNTS
   DOWN.
```

Variables are names used to represent values that will change during the course of a program. For example, a variable named D$ might represent any day of the week. It may help you to think of a variable as a storage box, waiting to receive whatever information you want to put in. Variables that deal with strings of characters are always followed by a dollar sign. Variables that end in a percent sign always hold integers (whole numbers like 1, 2, 3, 500). Variables with a pound sign or no special character at the end hold numbers that may contain fractions. The number of characters allowed in a variable name varies from computer to computer.

PROGRAM 1: THE DECODER

Modifications for Other Micros

TI 99/4A — The TI uses SEG$ to get a part of a string instead of MID$. It works the same way.

```
100 I$=SEG$(C$,I,1)
120 P$=P$ & I$
170 K=ASC(SEG$(K$,J,1))-ASC("A")+1
220 P$=P$ & CHR$(P+ASC("A")-1)
```

Atari 400/800 — The Atari handles strings differently than most other microcomputers. Add this line to encoder or decoder program:

```
15 DIM K$(10),C$(255),P$(255),I$(1)
```

and change the following lines:

```
100 I$=C$(I,I)
120 P$(LEN(P$)+1)=I$
170 K=ASC(K$(J,J))-ASC("A")+1
220 P$(LEN(P$)+1)=CHR$ (P+ASC("A")-1)
```

What the Program Does

This is a decoder program Orion uses to decode the message from ACT.

How the Program Works

This decoder program uses a "key" to decode the secret message. A key is a special word that tells the program just how to decode each letter of a message.

To encode the message, we use a formula like this:

key = OPAL
msg = THIS IS YOUR MISSION
formula:

```
  OPAL OP ALOP OPALOPA   Key
—THIS IS YOUR MISSION —Text
______________________________
  UHRS FW BWTY NCVWRWA
```

(the encoded message)

The way the program works, the key is always the sum of the values of two other letters. One of the letters is the plaintext; the other is the encoded letter. The computer must deal with letters as numbers, so we tell it to add or subtract the ASCII values by using the ASC function.

Then we use the CHR$ function at line 220 to turn the numbers back into letters.

(*Note:* On some computers, this program won't work correctly if there are commas or colons in the message.)

Here's something really interesting about this program. It can *encode* your messages as well as *decode* them. The program works both ways. Try it and send electronic secrets to your friends. But remember, they need the program and the password (key).

PROGRAM 2: QWERTYCODE

Modifications for Other Micros

Atari — Make these changes:
Don't put quotes in lines 20 and 30.

```
 15 DIM A$(26),B$(26),C$(255),D$(1)
110 D$=C$(I,I)
130 IF D$ = A$(J,J) THEN 170
170 PRINT B$(J,J);
```

TI-99/4A — Make these changes:

```
110 D$=SEG$(C$,I,1)
130 IF D$= SEG$(A$,J,1) THEN 170
170 PRINT SEG$(B$,J,1);
```

What the Program Does

This program is the decoder program that Orion and Robin worked out for special messages. It works on a principle called "alphabetic substitution," which means that one letter is always substituted for another letter in the code. It is one of the simplest methods of encoding, or "encrypting," messages. The QWERTYCODE is based on the arrangement of the letters on a computer keyboard going down each column of keys from left to right.

(The program is called QWERTYCODE because the top row of letters reads QWERTY on a keyboard.)

How the Program Works

First we put our two DATA statements in. They contain the mixed-up alphabet and a regular alphabet. We read these two alphabets into A$ and B$. Then we get our message from the person at the keyboard. That goes into the variable C$.

Next, for each letter of our message, which we get at lines 100 and 110, we check to see if it is in the regular alphabet. If it isn't, we just print it as it is. If it is in the alphabet, we print its corresponding letter from the mixed-up alphabet. That's all there is to it.

By the way, you can change this program to *encode* your messages. It's very simple. All you need to do is switch the mixed-up alphabet, and the regular alphabet. The easiest way to do that is to change line 40 to this:

```
40 READ B$,A$
```

PROGRAM 3: THE VAULT LOCK

Modifications for Other Micros

Atari — Make these changes:

```
 15 DIM D$(100),T$(20)
 18 T$="               ":REM 15 SPACES
 90 GRAPHICS 0
240 POSITION 10,10
270 PRINT T$(1,13);H;":";M;":";S;"     "
290 PRINT T$(1,12);D$(D*9+1,D*9+9)
310 GRAPHICS 0
```

IBM — Make these changes:

```
 90 CLS
240 LOCATE 10,10
310 CLS
```

TRS-80 — Make these changes:

```
 90 CLS
240 PRINT @650;
310 CLS
```

Radio Shack Color Computer — Make these changes:

```
 90 CLS
240 PRINT @330;
310 CLS
```

TI-99/4a — Make these changes:

```
 90 CALL CLEAR
240 CALL CLEAR
290 PRINT TAB(12);SEG$(D$,D*9+1,9)
310 CALL CLEAR
```

Commodore 64 and VIC-20 — Make these changes ("<CLR>" is the CLR key):

```
 90 PRINT "<CLR>";
240 PRINT "<CLR>";
310 PRINT "<CLR>";
```

What the Program Does

This program simulates a time lock on a vault. It has been programmed to tick off the seconds slowly. Since computers do things very fast, we use a "wait loop" to slow things down a bit. A wait loop does nothing but "wait." It is usually a FOR:NEXT loop in BASIC. In this program, the wait loop is at lines 100 and 110. We count up to the number in the variable C before continuing with the program.

How the Program Works

We set the value of the variable C in line 60. It is the speed of the clock. We have set it to 10. Setting C to 10 slows down the clock by making it wait 10 rounds of the loop each time the clock clicks. Can you guess how to slow down the clock even more? You could make the 10 into an even larger number, like 750. How do you think you can make the clock run faster? Would making C a small number help?

Orion is able to discover a trapdoor in the vault's lock. Look at the variable N, the increment. It is set to 1 by the READ statement with the DATA we have now. If anyone lowers the value of C, though, the increment N is changed to 7 in line 80. That will speed things up even more, since increment is used to boost the count of seconds and minutes. That is the trapdoor. We can change the value of the variable C to force the vault to open much earlier than it should.

Change the value of C in line 60 to 0 and watch what happens!

PROGRAM 4: QWERTYBACK

What the Program Does

When Orion tried to decode Robin's message, some of it was still not decoded. This program, which is a modification of the QWERTYCODE program, decodes the rest of the message. Orion realized that Robin's fingers must have slipped to the right on the keyboard when typing in the message, so an A ended up as an S, an E as an R, and so on. This program will take the garbled text that was printed when you ran the QWERTYCODE program and de-garble it.

Here is the entire program. Lines 20 and 30 must each be typed as one line on your computer.

```
 10 REM QWERTYBACK
 20 DATA
    "SNVFRGHJOKL!!MP!WTDYIBECUX"
 30 DATA
    "ABCDEFGHIJKLMNOPQRSTUVWXYZ"
 40 READ A$,B$
 50 PRINT "TYPE 'STOP' TO END PROGRAM"
 60 PRINT
 70 PRINT "INPUT MESSAGE";
 80 INPUT C$
 90 IF C$ = "STOP" THEN 210
100 FOR I = 1 TO LEN(C$)
110 D$ = MID$(C$,I,1)
120 FOR J = 1 TO 26
```

```
130 IF D$ = MID$(A$,J,1) THEN 170
140 NEXT J
150 PRINT D$;
160 GOTO 180
170 PRINT MID$(B$,J,1);
180 NEXT I
190 PRINT
200 GOTO 70
210 END
```

IBM	Apple		Radio Shack		Commodore		TI	Atari
PC & PCjr	II+	IIe	TRS-80	Color	64	VIC-20	99/4A	400/800
✓	✓	✓	✓	✓	✓	✓		

This program will run as is on the computers checked on the chart above. See below for changes for Atari and TI.

Modifications for Other Micros

Atari — Make these changes:
Don't put quotes in lines 20 and 30.

```
 15 DIM A$(26),B$(26),C$(255),D$(1)
110 D$ = C$(I,I)
130 IF D$ = A$(J,J) THEN 170
170 PRINT B$(J,J);
```

TI-99/4A — Make these changes:

```
110 D$=SEG$(C$,I,1)
```

```
130 IF D$= SEG$(A$,J,1) THEN 170
170 PRINT SEG$(B$,J,1);
```

How the Program Works

If you look at QWERTYCODE, you will see that this program is the same except for one DATA statement. This time we want the program to change the mixed-up alphabet to the real one. We added some exclamation points and other symbols that may not be exactly like your keyboard, so that the program would run on more computers. If you use this program, you may still get one or two garbled letters but you should be able to read Robin's message. It reads: OH, NO. THEY'RE AFTER ME. I THINK IT'S BECAUSE OF THE WINNING TICKET I SENT YOU. GOT TO HIDE. ROBIN.

PROGRAM 5: AIR BOMB

Modifications for Other Micros

TI-99/4A — Make these changes:

```
 20 CALL CLEAR
170 FOR K = 1 TO 500
175 NEXT K
200 PRINT "      "
205 NEXT L
210 PRINT (32000-1000*I)
230 PRINT "---------------+-- 16000"
```

Atari — Make these changes:

```
15 DIM S$(20),T$(25)
20 GRAPHICS 0
```

IBM and Color Computer — Make this change:

```
20 CLS
```

Commodore 64 and VIC-20 — Make this change:

```
20 PRINT "<CLR>" :REM USE THE CLR KEY
```

VIC-20 — Make these changes:

```
210 PRINT (32000-1000*I)/1000
230 PRINT
      "================+==16"
```

What the Program Does

This program simulates the control program for the computerized bomb in the airplane you are in.

How the Program Works

At line 70 you can see that there should be a way to deactivate the bomb. The deactivation code in the program starts at line 260. The trouble is, there is a bug in the program. Look at the program. Do you see which word should deactivate the bomb? (*Hint:* It's the bad guys!)

You probably found the secret word in line

90, an IF:THEN statement that checks for the deactivation word. If you answer with the right word, which line does the program go to? If you answer with the wrong word, where does the program go? Uh-oh, looks like it goes to line 100 either way. It should go to the deactivation phase if the word matches!

You can save the ACT team and all the people on board if you correctly change the IF:THEN statement in line 90, to go to line 260, then rerun the program. Be sure to enter the deactivation word when asked.

PROGRAM 6: SONOGRAM

What the Program Does

The SONOGRAM program analyzes the results of readings taken from the ACT sonograph machine. The readings were taken along two sides of the cave, one reading every meter. The X readings were taken along the south wall and the Y readings were taken along the east wall. This program looks for the intersection of the highest readings on the two walls. The intersection is where the X reading is the highest and the Y reading is the highest. The program then draws a chart of the cave and shows exactly where Robin should be located. It also prints this information to the screen.

To use the program, type in each of the

10 values for the X readings and each of the values for the Y readings, one at a time, when asked.

How the Program Works

The program gets 10 values for X. After getting each value, it decides whether or not that value is the highest so far. If it is, then the position of that value is stored in N. That means that if the third value is the highest, the number 3 is stored in N.

We do the same thing for each of the 10 values for Y. This time the position of the highest value is stored in the variable P.

That gives us all the information we need. It tells us Robin's position, in meters, from the two walls we measured.

PROGRAM 7: GRIDSUP

Modifications for Other Micros

Atari — The Atari deals with strings differently than most micros. That is why there are a lot of changes listed for it. (Line 100 has four spaces between quotes; line 110 has five.)

```
 15 DIM A$(50),B$(50),C$(50),Q$(10)
 20 GRAPHICS 0
 90 A$(LEN(A$)+1) = "----!"
100 B$(LEN(B$)+1) ="    !"
```

```
110 C$(LEN(C$)+1) = “     ”
130 A$(LEN(A$)+1) = “!”
140 B$(LEN(B$)+1) = “!”
150 C$(LEN(C$)+1) = “ !”
350 GRAPHICS 0
```

VIC-20 — Make these changes:

```
 20 PRINT “<CLR>”:REM USE CLR KEY
 30 W = INT(20/5)
350 PRINT “<CLR>”:REM USE CLR KEY
```

Commodore-64 — Make these changes:

```
 20 PRINT “<CLR>”:REM USE CLR KEY
350 PRINT “<CLR>”:REM USE CLR KEY
```

IBM — Make these changes:

```
 20 CLS
 30 W=INT(76/5)
350 CLS
```

TRS-80 — Make these changes:

```
 20 CLS
 30 W=INT(60/5)
350 CLS
```

Radio Shack Color Computer — Make these changes:

```
 20 CLS
 30 W=INT(28/5)
350 CLS
```

TI-99/4A — Make these changes (line 100 has four spaces between quotes; line 110 has five):

```
 20 CALL CLEAR
 30 W=INT(28/5)
```

```
 90 A$ = A$ & "-----!"
100 B$ = B$ & "     !"
110 C$ = C$ & "      "
130 A$ = A$ & "!"
140 B$ = B$ & "!"
150 C$ = C$ & " !"
350 CALL CLEAR
```

What the Program Does

This program makes a gate on the screen. When the correct code is typed, the grid will raise. Otherwise, the grid lock will be sealed. The entry code is 51.

How the Program Works

GRIDSUP is an example of simple animation done with text. Animation means that something appears to move. In this case, it is the gate.

GRIDSUP builds a gate with exclamation marks and hyphens and spaces. When the gate is raised, the program prints just the edges of the gate with spaces in between.

The variable N is used to control the height of the gate. The variable W controls the width of the gate. Since some computers have larger screens than others, this is an easy way to *customize* the program. To customize means to make changes to the program so that it will run better on any one computer.